The Arrow Stone

by

Michael A. Fenty

First published November 2020

Acknowledgements

Thanks to Gilly Becket for initial comments on style and presentation.
Thanks to Allan Simmons, Michelle Main and Marietta Fenty for editing and proofreading.
Thanks also to Michelle Main for help bringing it to publication.

Cover image by Allan Simmons.

Author's Note

Although some of the characters in the tale of the Arrow Stone did exist and many of the historical events referred to did take place, this remains a work of fiction and, other than verified historical facts, any resemblance to persons alive or dead or events described, is purely coincidental.

Introduction

On the Berwickshire coast, perched on its promontory high above the grey waters of the North Sea, Fast Castle has always been a place of mystery.

Its origins are obscure and its builders unknown. It guards no township or road, could easily be bypassed by an invading army and yet it has been fought over and changed hands many times since the first record of it in the fourteenth century. Scots and English armies have attacked, defended and garrisoned it. Great families, the Dunbars, Homes and Logans have all sought to possess it.

It has hosted royalty. Margaret Tudor stayed there en route to her marriage to James IV and the granddaughter of that union, Mary Queen of Scots, was a guest of the Homes there in 1566. The English ambassador, Throckmorton, described it as "very little yet very strong".

It has always been known to guard a secret.

Over the centuries many have searched for it.

Its erstwhile owner, the dissolute Robert Logan, entered into a contract with John Napier, the Wizard of Merchiston, inventor of logarithms to "do his utmost diligence to search and seek out, and by all craft and ingine to find out the same, and by the grace of God either find out the same, or make it sure that no such thing has been there."

The contract, written in Napier's own hand, still exists but no discovery was ever made.

Now ruinous, the castle has guarded its secret…until now.

Cup and ring marked stones and stone sculptures in the southern counties of Scotland

"...the last general list of rock carvings covered appeared in 1882 when fourteen sites were listed. In the present list, excluding those removed to museums, there are one hundred and eighty sites. This total was sub-divided into those on immoveable sites such as rock faces, and those on moveable sites, the rationale being that those on moveable sites may have been moved since carving.

The sites were analysed as to content whether they contained cup-and-ring; cup-only; ring-only; cup-and-ring or cup-only or ring-only with additional linear features; additional non-geometric, symbolic figures such as serpents, deer, fish etc. This latter type is very rare in this area.

One carving is unique in that it contains a non-geometric, non-symbolic figure namely an arrow. The so-called Arrow Stone is classed in the moveable group. At one time it formed part of the doorway to Templehall House, Coldingham though its original site is unknown. The house was destroyed by fire in 1946. The stone now forms part of a wall within the area northwest of St. Abbs Head."

Extract from the Proceedings of the Berwickshire Archaeology Soc. Vol. III Ch.14

CHAPTER 1

The Watcher didn't move. He could see the strangers making their way through the dense woodland. He could hear their speech though he did not understand it. Shapes formed in his mind - patterns, ideas. They were like him, these strangers, but not him. Their thoughts came to him in a way he could feel but not fully comprehend. They had a different colour, texture, a different dimension to those he was used to receiving from his own people. Speech wasn't always necessary within his tribal group. Ideas would spread through the families like ripples, each understanding in his or her own way what was required of them.

Words were used in the telling of stories around the fire, in the reciting of tribal histories and lore and of family genealogies. They were part of the formal gatherings when the scattered clans gathered to arrange large scale hunts of the great beasts that provided so much of their sustenance in food, hides for clothes and shelter, horn and bone for tools. There had to be invocations to the gods of the hunt and the spirits of the prey. For these occasions, speech was necessary but for the most part, thoughts were sufficient.

The strangers moved on through the forest. They looked like his people but were more lithe, moving with grace and agility, talking as they walked, gesturing as they talked. They appeared unafraid and confident and unaware of the signs of his people in the landscape that one of his kind would have read instantly. After they passed he waited and, there being no others, he made his way back to his family. He kept the encounter to himself to see if anyone else reported a similar occurrence, but none did.

Later, there was a gathering of the tribes at a sacred spot, a high flat rocky outcrop, to plan the seasonal migration to new hunting grounds following the herds that were already on the move. The smooth surfaces of the stones were marked with the symbols of his people's relationship to the land and the great Earth Mother.

That night, he knew he would have to mount to the sky and travel the silver arch of the stars across the dome of the cosmos. He had to go to the domain of the gods and bring back their blessing on his people's move. Fungi and plants were boiled together and strained. He drank the brew and, to the accompaniment of low chanting from the gathered tribe, he undertook his journey to try and see round the curve of time.

The alkaloids took effect and he travelled along the star path across the sky. His mind saw things he could not grasp, times beyond his time but one thing was clear. His people were not there, only the strangers.

He did not tell anyone what he had seen.

When the clan returned from its journey to the seasonal hunting grounds and sought to establish itself in familiar surroundings, the strangers were there again. His people had no concept of ownership of the land. It was simply where they had lived, with their seasonal wanderings for all time, given to them by the Earth Mother.

There was a wariness of the interlopers, but the Earth Mother was generous. The land was vast, the forests were rich in game and they were few. There was plenty for all so, at first, the two kept their distance from each other. There were contacts, sometimes cautiously friendly, sometimes angry, occasionally violent, but these were rare.

The Watcher grew old, his powers diminished, and he tried to pass on his skills, but none could match his abilities to reach the infinite and to convey the message of the Great Spirit. The tribe had to subsist with lesser gods. When he died, they buried him with full ritual in the recesses of the deepest cave where he would watch over them and his strengths and powers lived on in communal memory for the millennia that followed.

All retained the ability to feel the thoughts of others, to communicate without speech. This was in their genes, part of their self but few had the reach to go beyond their own time, that reach that had so troubled the Watcher.

Generations passed and the strangers became more numerous. Contacts were commoner, trading occurred, the taking of mates, sometimes by force, on both sides, the theft of children, disputes over hunting grounds. The people turned to their shamans for advice, but they could no longer climb to the arch of the sky as the Watcher had done.

The weather changed even within a lifetime, familiar prey disappeared and, as they followed the herds in their traditional hunts, they had to go further and returning each season became more and more arduous. The strangers seemed to deal with these problems with greater ease, their children seemed more numerous and some females, seeing this, left the tribe to join them causing further disputes with raids and counter-raids.

The bones of the Watcher were dug up and bought to the tribal council.

As the shaman held the skull he could feel the power of it pulsing through him. He could feel what had been lost. It was part of his nature, in his very being. It just needed releasing. Holding the skull, with its power, he too could see round the curve of time. He too felt the curse of that knowledge as had the Watcher, generations before.

He knew they must go, leave the ancestral lands, theirs for millennia, and move to where the sun set. He kept the rest to himself, as had the Watcher.

Before the tribe moved, they re-buried the bones in the cave. The shaman stood over them as they dug and then, with reverence, he placed the skull back into the ground, into the arms of the Earth Mother. He had thought to take it with them, but he had seen what the Watcher had seen all those generations ago and had carried silently, imparting to no-one, that vision of the future. Now the shaman would bear the same burden, the knowledge that they would be supplanted by the strangers and that their entire race would disappear from the face of the Earth. He too would carry that to his death. He and the skull and the legend of the Watcher would be forgotten as the struggle for survival played out.

Each generation found it harder than the previous one to succeed in the hunt. The climate turned colder, and the forests gave way to taiga and tundra. The great herds dwindled, familiar plants disappeared and always the strangers were there. Larger groups with more children, making more demands on resources. They seemed more able to deal with the changes and, more and more often, the females would drift off to join the groups of young males on the edges of the tribes of the strangers. Over years, the divisions became blurred but still the new peoples dominated, and the Watcher's people moved farther and farther west and north to the shores of the great ocean and to the islands of that ocean until they vanished from the globe.

The strangers, adaptive, communicative, procreative, fecund, became the masters of all they surveyed. Unopposed, they spread throughout the lands even to the shores and the islands of the great ocean.

The first people had gone but the millennia of contact had left a legacy in the strangers. Many carried the genes of the first people, diluted but still present, and some carried those of the Watcher and his kind.

CHAPTER 2

The executive coach was heading south down the A1 dual carriageway at well below the permitted speed. This was partly to ensure the comfort of the passengers who had paid highly for the privilege of not only visiting as many historical sites as possible in their day trip but also viewing at least as many more through the windows of the well-appointed vehicle with the added voice commentary from the tour guide.

EBBA Discovery tours - East Borders Bespoke Archaeology Discovery tours – specialised in providing whistle-stop trips around as many archaeological and historic sites as it was possible to see in one day with a highly qualified and personable guide to give a running commentary and answer any queries. It was designed to appeal to a retired, professional, financially sound clientele with an abiding interest in all things ancient or, at least, historic.

Each trip could be tailored to individual or group interests, prehistoric, medieval, and industrial or a mixture of all.

'Once again, may I congratulate those of you who made the ascent of Traprain Law? It does provide one of the best views in East Lothian. For those who chose the alternative visit to Hailes Castle, I'm sure you found that equally interesting. You've had a pretty full day, so we won't be stopping again until we reach

Coldingham which is our base for tomorrow's excursion but if there are any interesting places on the route, I'll point them out as we pass.'

David Morton swung round, switched off his microphone and relaxed into the front seat of the coach as it made its way to the final destination on the tour. Dry from talking all day, he popped a sweet into his mouth and picked up his sheaf of scribbled *aides memoires.*

He liked the job. By and large, the paying customers were polite and respected his knowledge or, at least, gave him the benefit of the doubt. Given the educational background of most of the passengers, some of them could have done a passable version of several of his topics themselves and, between them, could probably have managed the whole lot but they were in receptive mood and content to be spoon-fed little titbits of history as they chatted to one another and enjoyed the day out.

'We are just passing Doon Hill on the left, a settlement dating to the days before Scotland existed when all this area was part of the Anglian kingdom of Northumbria. We're not stopping. To be honest there isn't much to see. The site is just marked out on the ground. Oh yes, and over there just beyond the cement works, where they were quarrying for limestone to make cement, an excavation found the remains of a Mesolithic house. The oldest house in Scotland.'

'Excuse me,' came a voice from the body of the coach. 'Did you say Mesolithic... not Neolithic?'

'Yes Mesolithic. 12700 BC…or BCE as we tend to say nowadays. Nearly fifteen thousand years ago. There was another discovered at Cramond on the Firth of Forth and another down the coast in Northumberland, at Howick.'

Another voice, slightly hesitant as if afraid of sounding stupid, came from the seats further back.

'Is there any sign of Neanderthals in any of the excavations in this area?'

'No. No,' replied David in a voice that implied that this was a reasonable question and should be treated as such.

'You have to go back much, much further, beyond the last Ice Age, for Neanderthals. They seemed to have died out about 40,000 years ago and most of our knowledge about them comes from southern Europe, Spain and Gibraltar and the Middle East, Israel, Syria, Jordan. That part of the world. They may never have lived here.'

He paused, thinking how he might make the woman feel that her question wasn't so wide of the mark. After all, he was paid to be nice to everyone and to make them all feel part of the experience.

'But, here's a thought. When the scientists sequenced the genome of the Neanderthals, they reckoned that Europeans have up to two percent Neanderthal DNA in their make-up. Although there is no evidence of Homo Neanderthalensis in Scotland any one of us could have traces of those ancient folk. Maybe some more than others.'

He sank back into his seat thinking that would keep them discussing and chattering amongst themselves for the rest of the trip.

After a few miles, he felt he really ought to earn his corn and, at the same time create a link to the next stop at Coldingham Priory.

'I know it sounds a bit banal to draw your attention to the sheep grazing on the moorlands, but they do just remind us that the Scottish Borders is sheep rearing country, quite different from the arable lands of Lothian that we've just left. Saint Cuthbert himself is said to have been a shepherd boy in the Lammermuirs. All the great Border abbeys, Kelso, Melrose Jedburgh, grew rich on the wool trade either directly or from tithes on the sheep farmers, and Coldingham was no exception. It was one of the wealthiest foundations in Scotland and had trading links with the continent, particularly the Low Countries. The monks have long gone, and Coldingham Priory is just an interesting ruin, but the sheep still graze the moors.'

On that descriptive flourish, he sat back in his seat. He did like to add a bit of theatre to his talks.

CHAPTER 3

Bahis was thirsty. He tended the family's small herd of goats and fat-tailed sheep as they wandered over the dry ground foraging for what little pasture they could find. Scrubby trees dotted the landscape, protecting their leaves with sharp thorns yet the nimble and persistent goats managed to browse even on them.

Surveying his charges, he realised the little brown one with the curious white mark on her back was missing. She was so distinctive; he couldn't mistake her. He scanned the surrounding rocks and sand, but she was nowhere to be seen. Calling to her, he scrambled up a pile of large boulders flanking the escarpment that overlooked the valley where they grazed. He had given all his charges pet names, something he didn't divulge to the older members of his family fearing they would make fun of him.

Losing one of the herd would be bad enough, arousing the anger of his father and the scorn of his elder brothers but even more so was the loss of his favourite. His stomach tightened into a knot as he called

'Fariha! Fariha!'

There was a cleft in the rock face with a shelf covered in wind-blown sand. He saw her neat, almond shaped hoof prints picked out in a delicate tracery across the sand. His heart lifted and he hauled himself onto the ledge. There she was, looking at him with her yellow eyes, giving a soft bleat of recognition.

'You rascal. What are you doing here? There's nothing for you to eat here.'

Then he noticed the entrance to the cave. Partially covered by a rock fall, it seemed to beckon him.

He approached hesitantly. Snakes, scorpions and other dangers were to be found in caves. Jinns too could be lurking in caves. He was fearful yet he felt drawn to enter. Searching around the rocks, he scraped together a few tumbleweeds of dry branches from the zilla thorn. He twisted them into a crude torch. Squeezing past the great boulder masking the entrance, he searched in his pouch for some of the downy hairs gathered from the spiny thistle and a flint and steel.

One expert strike and a spark glowed in the downy bundle. Blowing gently, he nursed it into the midst of the dry branches. Holding his brand in front as a guide and a defence, he advanced into the cave. The flickering light on the walls and the deep dark recesses that could hold any terror, made his hair prickle on his neck, yet he felt compelled to search further.

As his simple light started to fail, he made the furthest reach of the cave and was about to turn back out when his foot caught on something on, or more accurately, in, the sandy floor. Bending down he saw the domed vault of a skull protruding from the ground with the empty eye sockets looking at him. He froze, his throat dry and closing in a silent scream of fear. A Jinn, an earth-demon. He turned to flee, waving his torch around his head in terror. As he did so, it flared into life and he saw the skull for what it was. Tentatively, he reached down and pulled it from the grip of the earthen floor of the cave.

Whatever tremor had brought down the rock fall across the cave mouth at some time in the millennia since the days of the Watcher's people, had thrust the skull from its sacred resting place into the dry air of the surface. Bahis held it up but his torch flame died before he could examine his find so, carrying it in a fold of his robe, he scrambled back into the bright sunlight of the surface.

He held the skull at arm’s length and looked into the empty eye sockets. He was no longer afraid of it but something about it caused him to shiver and he felt as if it was looking at him, searching for something. He made a fold in his djellaba and driving his errant goat before him he returned to round up the rest of his small herd and headed for his father's tents.

At first his parent was angry. Perhaps his son had defiled a tomb, shown lack of respect for the dead but, as Bahis described the circumstances, his grandfather spoke on his behalf. He said that there were many strange places in the desert land and many people had lived there long before their own people had come. He himself had seen drawings in caves of animals, and creatures that did not live there now and of people.

The skull must have come from the old times long, long ago, from even before the days of the patriarchs. He remarked on its strange shape.

'It is not as the skull of a man such as we. It must be from a time in the past, perhaps from before the great flood. From those that perished then perhaps?'

Bahis noticed that, as they passed it around, they did not seem to suffer the involuntary tremor he had felt but then he thought nothing of it.

As Bahis slept that night the older men discussed his find and the eldest of them decreed that it should be presented to the tribal leader to decide on its fate.

Thus, from the trembling hands of a small boy the skull began its journey through clan leader to local sheik to the atabeg of the region, Imad ad-Din Zengi.

CHAPTER 4

'Well, ladies and gentlemen, the final part of today's tour. Here in the ruins of the Coldingham Priory you can wander around and explore as much as you like. The present-day church is based on the choir of the original Priory which covered most of the churchyard you see around you. The church is open, and you can see the remaining north wall with its intact stonework.'

David led the group into the kirkyard surrounding the remains of Coldingham Priory, talking as he walked and pointing out various features.

'Before that, I would draw your attention to this odd collection of stones which has been called the lapidarium. When this place was destroyed by Cromwell's forces in the civil war after the revolution and the execution of Charles the First. The villagers, with an eye for an opportunity, used the ruins as a handy quarry to build houses, dykes, anything that was needed. If you stroll round the village you'll see bits of dressed and ornamental stone incorporated into nearly every house. There wasn't any concept of what we would now call conservation but, despite that, there was a recognition that some stones were special, to be treated with respect, maybe even fear.

These special stones were kept apart and later they were built into this crazy wall. If you look carefully, you can see what may have been a stone piscina from the first Anglo-Saxon church, a green man, a pagan belief surviving conversion to Christianity and, most renowned, the Templar crosses.'

At the mention of the Knights Templar, his audience gathered round to inspect the weathered slabs, grave coverings with their stepped crosses accompanied by a long sword and dagger. This was even more exciting than the stream of Iron Age forts, medieval saints, plague pits and stories of wrecks that they had experienced on this day of the whirlwind trip round east coast of Scotland antiquities that comprised the EBBA Discovery Tour.

As well as tours by coach to historic houses, castles and battlefields with appropriate commentary *en route*, select groups of enthusiasts were transported in a converted Landrover Discovery cross country, along cliff tops and over field and stream to visit and experience the more remote sites of this ancient land from the Mesolithic to the Industrial Revolution with the guide adding background detail and colour to them. A field trip in a comfortable seat.

David Morton reflected that he did like this job. Despite its disadvantages, short contract and not the greatest pay packet, it appealed to the teacher in him. It required a certain amount of acting to appear enthusiastic and interested for every new group asking the same questions and giving him the benefit, as they saw it, of their own ideas. He took it all with a geniality that was mostly natural but a bit professional. Each trip was a fresh experience for them that wouldn't be repeated so he had to act and make it as memorable for the last customers of the season as it was for the first.

The group twittered and whispered amongst themselves as they clustered round the assemblage of stones. One elderly lady, he had mentally labelled as a retired school teacher, approached him.

'How do we know these are anything to do with the Knights Templar?'

He had been over this ground before. The explosion of interest in this particular monastic order with best-selling novels, films and video games had spawned so many theories and conclusions that most people with a serious interest in history had a default cynicism at the mere mention of the name.

'Well, we don't know is the real answer though there is a local tradition about the grave slabs that dates back years and years, long before they became known to wider public, as it were. There is a farm near here called Templehall and there was a big house and estate of that name as well. The house burned down in the 1940's and the estate has long been broken up. So, to answer your question, it is pure conjecture, but no-one has come up with a better explanation.'

He furrowed his brow in an effort of memory.

'...and there is a mention in a twelfth century manuscript of the Templars holding land at Auldcambus, a few miles north of here.'

The woman was not prepared to give up on her cross examination. She had paid for this trip and intended to extract the maximum amount of information from it.

'But why would they end up in this particular spot.'

David addressed the whole group, acting the part, involving them in the story, giving the account colour and drama, trying to transport his listeners to that time in this place.

'Why Coldingham? Indeed, why Coldingham? This was once one of the richest religious houses in Scotland. The Benedictine monks had established a thriving agricultural business with links to England and Europe. When Philip IV of France forced Pope Clement into declaring the Templars heretics and suppressing the order in 1313. One of their heresies was that they worshipped a "head" though it was never made clear what was meant by this. Some people conflated that with the Shroud of Turin which, if it were folded up, might just show the head but I think that's been well and truly discounted by now.'

He turned from the group.

'As I'm sure you know,' he went on, speaking directly to his original questioner, in a polite allusion to her obvious knowledge.

'Philip owed the Templars money and it was all a ruse to get out of his debts. He had form. He had expelled the Jews a few years before when he was owing them large sums of cash.'

She nodded to show that she too knew her medieval history.

'The Templars that could escape the arrests, fled and sought refuge with other orders such as the Benedictines.'

'But why here in particular?'

Morton became aware that the others in the group were hanging on his words. The school teacher had led him into a complex history lesson that he hadn't bargained for. Usually, a bit of general background was enough to keep the customers happy but not this lady. He took a breath and expanded his explanation, giving the company the full benefit of his background reading.

'Well, Robert the Bruce was fighting for supremacy in Scotland not just against Edward I of England but also against other claimants for the throne. He had murdered John Comyn, his greatest rival, in a church. For this, he was excommunicated by the Pope, but Bruce went on to claim the throne and was crowned King of Scots by the Bishop of Glasgow in defiance of the Pontiff's wishes.

In 1314, the Templars' Grand Master Jaques de Molay was burned alive as a heretic and many others were killed or imprisoned. Just as the Templars were helping the excommunicant Robert Bruce to consolidate his hold on the Scottish crown at the Battle of Bannockburn, their order was being systematically destroyed all over Europe.

It was clear that the rule of the Pope didn't hold much sway here so Templars would have felt safer in Scotland than in, say, England, France or Spain where they were persecuted, and it is easy to reach Coldingham by sea from France and England.'

The lady pursed her lips and considered his answer. Definitely, a retired teacher, he thought. Then she nodded and joined the rest of the listeners.

Probably a Gamma plus, he thought, a safe pass mark. No commendation for him.

He couldn't resist trying for a bonus point.

'Jacques de Molay may not have been a heretic but he seems to have been able to see into the future. He cursed the king and the pope and said they would be dead within a year and he was correct, and he predicted the fall of Philip's dynasty. The death of all the male heirs. That's some prediction, and it did all happen as he said it would.'

'Yes,' she replied. 'The so-called Accursed Kings.'

There was the slightest twitch of the mouth. She had recognised his effort. Perhaps he had managed a Beta.

'Let's go back to the bus. Your evening meal awaits and tomorrow I'll have more tales of jealousy and murder, then on to Edin's Hall Broch.'

He loaded his charges into their transport and returned them to the local hotel that served as a base for the historical weekend trip. Half board and packed lunches provided on request.

CHAPTER 5

Released from his tourist duties, David drove back to the cottage he rented up on the moors. One of the perks of the job was the Landrover Discovery that he drove to reach the historical sites too far from the roads to be approached on foot. It did mean that larger groups had to be split, and several trips were involved but it created a sense of adventure amongst the middle-aged history enthusiasts as they were ferried across heath and moor. For all personal use, any fuel consumed above the carefully calculated mileage of the trips was at his own expense.

In the cottage he could relax. He had mastered the intricacies of the slow cooker. Steak, carrots, onions and potatoes, chopped and seasoned had been simmering all day and now were ready for his evening meal. He was pleased with himself. Having lived as a single man dining in staff canteens and fast food outlets of every cuisine imaginable supplemented by the pop and ping of the microwave, he now prepared simple meals from local ingredients bought in local shops. He felt virtuous.

Life was pleasant. He had a job that wasn't taxing and for the most part enjoyable, he had comfortable accommodation in bucolic surroundings and, most importantly, he had enough free time to indulge his interest in the cup and ring marks of the sculptured stones found all over Europe, indeed some would say all over the world. He knew most people would find his interest boring or pointless, but from childhood walks in the hills with his father, he had been fascinated by these strange carvings.

As a boy he would sit on the flat rocks on the moors and trace the whorls and spirals with his finger. Who made them and why? What did they mean? His father couldn't tell him and just said that they were very old. Maybe they were from the Stone Age. In his comics, Stone Age men were always shown in skins with giant clubs living in caves but there were no caves near where they walked on the high moors.

It was only later in life that he learnt of the Palaeolithic, Mesolithic and Neolithic ages and the millennia that those eras took to pass and of how these people were just as clever as people were now and how they built their great stone monuments and had an understanding of time and space and their relationship to the natural world that could be described as religious or spiritual.

So why had they spent much of their precious time creating these puzzle pictures on the rocks and why, over how many thousands of years, had they been added to and embellished?

He had read every paper he could find in all the recognised scientific journals as well as the more bizarre theories on websites throughout the internet. The petroglyphs continued to fascinate him. He visited sites, photographed and sketched, made notes of position of carvings in relation to the surrounding geographic features, both immediate and in the wider landscape. He behaved like a complete anorak and he loved it. He had no fixed ideas about where all this collected data would lead him, if anywhere, but he didn't care. He was simply indulging himself. Some people collect stamps or coins or beer mats or get twitchy over rare bird sightings or go trainspotting. He collected petroglyphs. There were dozens scattered over the hills of the neighbouring county, close enough to visit in a day and every day off was spent driving round, map in hand, checking them off.

There was one elusive example. Recorded in the local antiquities list as the Arrow Stone, it fell into the category of moveable carvings.

Most cup and ring markings were on rock outcrops and were very obviously still in the same spot as when they were created but some were literally moveable, having been carved on boulders which may or may not be found in their original sites. Some of those found in Neolithic tombs were from earlier times and were moved and incorporated because they were recognised as sacred even if their original meaning had been lost.

The original site of the Arrow Stone was unknown. First, it had been listed as having formed the lintel over a doorway in the local mansion house called Temple Hall. How it had arrived there, no-one had recorded. It was reused stone. Possibly it had come from the ruins of the local Priory, destroyed by Parliamentarian troops when pressed into service as a Royalist stronghold in the Cromwellian civil war of the seventeenth century. Bits of dressed stone showing evidence of the medieval masons' skill could be found in the walls of many local buildings, large and small. The resourceful inhabitants had seen no reason to go and quarry anew when there was a plentiful supply on their doorstep.

It was assumed by the antiquarians listing the existence of the Arrow Stone that it had arrived for use as part of the stone brought from quarries further up the coast, hewn from its original site on some rock face, to build the medieval priory.

No other explanation seemed feasible.

Now it had been moved yet again. Temple Hall had burned down possibly due to an accident with a candle, and lives had been lost.

The blackened shell had been demolished and the stones reused once more. They were given a more mundane function as part of a field dyke somewhere in the area.

The location of the stone was mentioned in the transactions of the local antiquarian society, an august body of interested amateurs that had existed since the nineteenth century. Clergy, physicians, landowners, merchants had met regularly to listen to celebrated guest speakers and had meticulously investigated and catalogued not only the antiquities of the region but the flora, fauna and geology as well. This huge fund of information was contained in the bound volumes of records assiduously kept over many decades by Hon. Secs. to the Society. A group of men and occasionally, women who truly earned the title Honourable.

David had become fixated by the Arrow Stone. As a collector, he wanted this specimen in his logbook more than any other.

He intended to go to the location, find and photograph the stone and perhaps make a sketch or even a wax crayon rubbing.

Duty called. Business before pleasure. He had to check out Fast Castle as a site for the next group of tourists. The approach could be treacherous especially after the recent heavy rain. It didn't really count as business as he loved going there. The ruins of a keep perched on its rocky pinnacle with the cliffs falling sheer to the sea. What a spot to stir the imagination. No wonder Sir Walter Scott had used it as a model for Wolf's Crag in "The Bride of Lammermoor". He reckoned the steep descent would be too much for his middle-aged sightseers.

Come on, he thought. Who am I kidding? If they are middle-aged then they are going to live to be a hundred and fifty. They'll never manage down to the castle and even if they did, they wouldn't manage across the entrance. The castle was approached by a steep path leading to a narrow land bridge to the rocky pinnacle on which it stood. The rusting chains that provided handholds across the bridge were also used to hoist oneself over the last big outcrop into the castle itself. The sheer cliffs falling away on each side of the entrance made it not one for those with vertigo or a tendency to stumble.

No, he concluded to himself. I'll find a suitable parking place on the slope above the path where the castle is visible and hand round some binoculars. Pity though because it is a great place to actually get to and to sit and wonder at the skill of those who built it.

Driving along the single track road from the A1107, the "moors road" to the locals, he embraced the view across the Firth of Forth to the Kingdom of Fife on the opposite shore and on as far as the Grampian mountains. The fields around the road still bore the scars of bomb craters, the aftermath of the Luftwaffe's attempts to eliminate the radar station guarding the wartime coastline. In the uneasy peace that followed the grass and field weeds had reclaimed the ground, blurring the edges of the pits but the station had continued to scan the skies for a new enemy from the East. A huge underground facility had been created to warn of a nuclear attack that never came. This too had gone. The valves replaced by microcircuitry and the personnel by remote monitors. The cliff tops now had simple beacons and unmanned sensors that scarcely showed in the landscape, barely noticeable from the car window as the Discovery growled over cattle grids and dodged errant sheep.

He loved going to Fast Castle. He had been told by the locals that not so long ago puffins had nested there and also the story of a treasure, a secret treasure. He had laughed this off saying that such stories were ten a penny but had been assured that the idea had been taken seriously enough for John Napier, renowned mathematician and inventor of logarithms, to have been employed to try and find it. For centuries it had been sought with no-one quite knowing what it was they were seeking but firm in the knowledge that there was a secret, a treasure to be found.

Who built the keep? Why was it built there? Its origins were unrecorded, but it had been fought over, taken and retaken for centuries. It didn't appear to guard anything. The bleak moorland on the approach was of no value and the castle was too far from the road that crossed it to be an effective barrier to progress. The road couldn't even be seen from the castle but, perhaps more significantly, the castle couldn't be seen from the road. Clambering up the slippery rock at the entrance and standing in what would have been the courtyard of the old keep, he knew what the castle guarded and why it was there.

The sea.

That was its reason and purpose. From this point, probably since Palaeolithic times, the occupants of the promontory could see the approach of boats or ships from miles away. To his left, the volcanic plug that became the Bass, the great rocky gannet colony in the firth and the cone of Berwick Law were clearly visible and, across the sea, the Isle of May and the Fife coast with its fishing towns. That was why Fast Castle was here and why, in times when the seas were the highways, it had been so important. Even as he looked out, the cargo vessels bound for Leith, sailed along the horizon and the fishing boats stuttered their way along the coast dodging the rocks as the men hoisted up the pots or craves hoping for crabs and lobsters. Below the two hundred foot cliffs, seals lolled on the shingly beaches like huge slugs and shags and kittiwakes fished offshore in the white horses of the wave tips. He sat among the ruined walls and tumbled stones, letting his mind drift, feeling the sun on his face, watching the lines of gannets arrowing down from the Bass to their fishing grounds and keeping an eye out for a glimpse of the peregrine that swooped on the rock doves from the cliffs.

The stonework was a mixture of the old red sandstone and greywacke that made up the spectacular coastline, the folded strata of the latter lying like slices of bread piled up in great lines reaching out into the sea, a hazard for any vessel approaching the shore. Between the layers, caves formed with dark triangular mouths, caves fashioned by the rough tongue of the sea reaching into base of the great cliffs, tempting to the curious but treacherous with slippery passages and in-rushing tides. The clear deep waters held many wrecks, beloved of the new visitors, the sub-aqua clubs, but also a reminder of the deadly combination of wind, tidal currents and rock that made this a dangerous coast.

CHAPTER 6

The cog yawed and rolled in the swell of the North Sea as it rounded the head. Sturdy and high-sided, she coped with the crash of the seas on her wooden walls. The master, an experienced Freislander had plied these waters many times carrying iron, ceramics and glass to the port of Leith and returning with wool and salt fish for the Flemish market. Scottish merchants had a market in Bruges and links into the trade routes as far as Poland and Sicily.

The south easterly currents and the steep cliffs with their promontories and outliers where the seas boiled and seethed would have usually meant the wary captain giving this coastline a wide berth, but tonight he had an extra cargo and an unusual destination.

He had been well paid, very well paid. Enough coin to keep his crew quiet and his own pocket filled. He had to watch for a light. This in itself was a danger, for wreckers used the same ruse to lure ships to the rocks. Not for nothing had the laird of Auldcambus been known as Edward the Wrecker and been sentenced to death a century before. He had only escaped the axe by transferring his lands to Bertram, the Prior of Coldingham. Wreckers still carried out their villainous trade along that coast, but the captain had been reassured that those who would show the light were such that no wrecker would dare trespass on their domain and the man who told him and the manner in which he was told, left no doubt in his mind that it was true.

The cog crept along beneath the towering cliffs, her crew muttering fearfully of such a venture, their senses taut waiting to hear the scream of the timbers as a rock tore the bottom from their vessel. Then, turning into the shelter of a bay, they saw high above them a beacon, an iron basket of tarred wood flaring in the wind. By its light, they could see the stone walls of a castle tower rising out of the cliff itself. They could also see the black walls of sheer rock that enclosed the narrow approach and the arched mouth of the great cave at its end. The surge of the sea on the shingle in the entrance sucking like a huge mouth, seemed destined to consume the ship and the crew sweated with fear.

The captain eased the flat bottomed cog beneath the light and dropped anchor. Holding his vessel steady into the wind, he shouted to lower the square rigged sail and waited.

High above, a great wooden arm swung out from the battlement and a basket on ropes creaked slowly down to the deck. As the basket settled on the deck, the door of the stern castle opened, and the crew caught their first and last sight of the cargo that had earned them the extra pay and the nerve-racking detour to the Scottish coast. Two tall, heavily built men with weathered faces and the erect demeanour of soldiers emerged carrying a chest between them. Beneath their brown mantles could be seen the black tunic of the Order of Saint Benedict, the Benedictines, the Black Monks. A more acute observer might have discerned that they were also armed, their broadswords hanging beneath their mantles. Only pausing to raise their cowls against the wind swept spray, they climbed into the wicker basket, gave a tug on the signal rope and were hoisted into the night.

The captain held the rudder over hard and cautiously raised the sail. The sturdy little ship was remarkably responsive, and they cleared the bay and headed out away from the coast. Looking back, they could see no sign of the light or the castle and, dismissing the incident from their minds, they thought no more of it as they sailed on to their usual port of call.

The basket bumped down and on the forecourt of the castle and hands helped the men over the sides but any assistance with the chest was firmly if politely refused and they continued to carry it between them as they were escorted to the hall.

A fire warmed the stone-walled chamber which was simply but adequately furnished. A man in the robes of the Benedictines and wearing a large pectoral cross set with an amethyst, rose from the chair by the fire and extended his hand.

'Brothers, welcome to Fast Castle.'

In the warmth of the fire, the two men shed their surcoats and revealed the red cross over the left side of their tunics, over their hearts. The red cross of martyrdom, the cross of the Poor Fellow-Soldiers of Christ and of the Temple of Solomon, more commonly called The Knights Templar.

The Prior spoke the lingua franca of the order, a form of Provençal and Frankish but when the broad Yorkshire vowels which betrayed his origins perplexed his listeners, he changed into Latin, the universal language of the church.

'We have been expecting you since we received news of the dreadful events in France. Warm yourselves by the fire and refresh yourselves, then we will hear all the details. We are still under the rule of Durham, and thus that of Edward Plantagenet, but changes are afoot. The Bruce was excommunicated by his Holiness but absolved by Bishop Wishart of Glasgow and crowned King of Scotland. His excommunication means that the Pope's writ doesn't always run in this realm and we, while maintaining our obedience to the Holy See, as you would expect, await events. Many of your fellow brethren have found shelter in Scotland and the king has found use for their expertise. You are safe here. This castle has been in the possession of the Priory since Prior Bertram's time and has proved useful on more than one occasion. I see you have brought a chest with you. I will not question its contents at present but if it contains what I suspect it does, then even this redoubt, remote and unvisited as it is, is not safe enough.

When we are sure that your arrival has not been noted, we will move you to more comfortable quarters in Coldingham where your order already has a property. What is the correct term?'

'We call all our properties "houses" regardless of their status or size.' said one of the travellers. 'We like simplicity.'

'Indeed,' beamed the prelate. 'May I examine the... ahem... cargo?'

The traveller's gloved hand came down firmly on the lid of the box.

'We would prefer not.'

'As you please.' replied his host somewhat peevishly.

CHAPTER 7

Faced with lugging her heavy trunk from her car to the rented cottage, Katherine Donaldson looked round for someone to help but no-one was about. I could do with a couple of sturdy fishermen, she thought. Just my luck. Not a soul.

She had parked across the road from the cottage in what would have been a kitchen garden in the days when the row of cottages was occupied by fishermen and their families. Now, they were holiday homes and the little cabbage patches had become parking spaces and, as she had discovered, fishermen were scarce.

It had seemed like a good idea at the time to put all her gear into one large case but now she thought better of it. She dragged it into the tiny hallway and sat on it surveying her new home for the summer. A sitting room simply but adequately furnished and, craning round the door, she could see a small kitchen beyond. The hallway ended in a bathroom of sorts and presumably up the short narrow stairs were the two bedrooms, as advertised, though one at least must qualify only by reason that it contained a bed and not much else. It seemed scarcely believable that within living memory a whole family with several children had lived in this cramped little cottage; *just* within memory it was true, but nevertheless. She felt a little chastened by the thought and immediately solved her problem with the case by dint of opening it in the hall and dispersing the contents to the most suitable parts of the tiny dwelling.

Unloading the kayak from the roof rack would require assistance but that could wait.

Time enough for chores, she decided to explore the village of St Abbs perched on the slope above a little harbour so quaint and picturesque it looked as if it had been designed for the tourist trade not the hard world of seafaring.

There were fewer working boats now and they were mostly small craft setting pots or "craves" for crab and lobster but there were men around who had fished the Arctic for cod and some who had gone further to the southern oceans in the days of the whaling fleets. Kate strolled about taking in the views that had featured as a backdrop for television and film dramas. Strangers were not unusual in the tourist season but an attractive young woman with a mane of red hair was always going to be noticed. Kate was used to it and, to a certain extent, enjoyed the glances from the passing male population.

David Morton had taken a break from his seemingly endless task of checking every stone on Northfield and, with thought to his newly acquired culinary skills, was making his way into the village to the weekly market. Time I tried out some fish dishes, he thought. Too much meat is not the healthiest option. Time I got some omegas into the diet.

He was mulling over the decision to go for mussels and try his increasing culinary skills on *moules mariniere* or settle for the traditional Scottish smoked fish with poached egg when he saw Kate.

Not a local delicacy, he thought and quickly rehearsed in his mind a few opening gambits. Living alone and lecturing to the middle aged and elderly had dulled his socialising skills. He felt gauche and clumsy.

'Hello. You're new.' he blurted out.

Kate turned and gave him a cool, appraising look.

'Well, not brand new,' she grinned.

'Sorry, that was rude of me, but we don't see... I haven't seen you here before,' he stammered.

'Maybe that's because I haven't been here before.' she teased then, feeling sorry for his embarrassment, added, 'I've just moved into one of the cottages above the harbour.'

She paused and looked him up and down. He wasn't a burly fisherman, but he looked fit enough.'You could help me get my kayak off the car roof.'

'Of course. No problem,' he replied, relieved at not being rebuffed.

'Now?'

'No hurry, finish whatever you're doing. Buying fish?'

'Yes, planning my supper.'

'I live on my own,' he added by way of explanation or information. He wasn't sure which but, buoyed up with confidence, he seized the initiative. After all, she had asked for his help.

Making a show of looking at his watch, he said, 'Talking of food, I was going to have some lunch down at the harbour. Would you like to join me?'

Kate looked at him. He was, to use a dated term, chatting her up, but he looked and sounded agreeable. She was hungry, there was still the matter of the kayak and lunch in a public place seemed an acceptable suggestion so, all in all, why not?

'Sounds like a good idea.'

He settled for the smoked fish and they set off down the hill to the little restaurant on the harbour front with its chalked blackboard of daily "specials".

Over bowls of Cullen skink, they exchanged details of themselves. David explained his short term career as a tour guide and then, somewhat shyly, his interest in the petroglyphs and his local search for the Arrow Stone. He had been used to a bored response to his mentioning his pet project. Most people couldn't comprehend his enthusiasm for squiggles on stones but to his surprise, Kate genuinely seemed interested.

'I'm here to do a bird count on the reserve. Sea birds primarily, but all the birds I come across. If

I come across your Arrow Stone on my travels, I'll mark the spot and pass it on.'

'Counting birds? Sounds a bit difficult. They don't tend to sit still for long.'

Kate laughed.

'No indeed. We rarely go one, two, three. Oh dear, that one's moved. No, there are various proven techniques and there is usually a trade-off between complete accuracy and practicality. On a cliff, say, you could study some sample areas and extrapolate from them to the whole colony, or you can count groups in areas defined by rock features like ledges and add them together. Sometimes we use nest site mapping. There are lots of different ways of doing it.'

'So I've heard.' He risked a joke.

To his relief, Kate laughed.

'Oh you are awful,' she retorted in a mock-offended voice.

'I hope the rest of the male population around here aren't as quick on the uptake as you are.'

'Sorry, it just came out.' He reddened slightly. 'Sorry.'

Kate rose from the table.

'Let's pay before you get in more trouble,' she said. 'You've still got to help with the kayak.'

As they walked back to her cottage, David thought, all things considered, things had gone rather well for a chance encounter. Kate thought the summer job might not be all work after all.

CHAPTER 8

Rigaud was born in Aachen in the centre of the Holy Roman Empire, the legacy of the great Charlemagne. He was brought up on stories of how Charles Martel had stopped the Saracens from invading Europe at the Battle of Tours and of how his grandson, the great Christian emperor, Charlemagne had created the empire of the Franks bringing almost all of Europe into his domain and how he had fought and defeated the Moors in Hispania.

Rigaud heard how the tall, fair haired emperor had defended Christendom against the Moslems and defeated the pagan Saxons. The tale of these exploits always excited him especially as his hero was said to have fair hair like his own. As he wielded his wooden sword, he imagined himself as Charlemagne.

He was ten years old when Peter the Hermit, in response to the Pope's plea, called upon everyone, not just the knights and soldiers, to join a People's Crusade to free the Holy Land from the grip of the Seljuk Turks. Fired with a youthful desire for adventure and wish to emulate his hero, Rigaud join the Crusade. In April 1096 he set off as part of a raggle-taggle army of forty thousand peasants and paupers, women and children, more a horde than an army that marched and slept, foraged and stole their way across Europe. Thirty thousand of them made it to Constantinople.

Rigaud was clever and had reserves of stamina and a will to survive that enabled him to escape starvation, servitude or being sold into slavery by the robber barons of the Balkans. He made it to the fabled Byzantium.

He marvelled at the sight of Constantinople, the magnificent city of the Byzantine empire and realised by comparison, what a poor place, for all its status, Aachen, was.

The great dome and spires of the Hagia Sophia dwarfed the Palatine Chapel of Aachen. The bustle and riches of the markets and stalls, the silks and spices, the candles, soaps, spices, precious metals and enamelled icons, were like a dazzling dream. Never could he have imagined such wealth, such finery and so much food.

Rigaud didn't have much time to assimilate the splendours of Byzantium. Appalled by this unruly mob of an army that had begun to pillage the countryside around his capital, Emperor Alexios Komnenos quickly arranged passage for them across the Bosporus encouraging them on to Jerusalem. Having little in the way of military skills and lacking leadership, as they marched through into the territory of the Seljuk Turks, they were massacred in encounter after encounter. The pitiful few that survived included Rigaud.

Of Peter's misguided volunteers who had set off so valiantly two years before, only a handful managed to join the force of trained knights and men-at-arms commanded by Stephen of Blois who had followed them to the Holy Land and were laying siege to Antioch, half way to Jerusalem. Peter was twelve years old but had marched across Europe and fought his way through the lands of the Turks. He felt he was a man.

Antioch was so large that the Crusaders could not fully blockade it and so the siege stuttered on and off with attacks from the Turks on the besiegers.

During one such attack by Kerbogha, the atabeg of Mosul, Rigaud was taken prisoner and brought back to Mosul as a slave. Intrigued by his fair hair and complexion, Kerbogha decide to give him to his adopted ward, Imad ad-Din Zengi. Zengi was a few years older than Rigaud.

'What is he called?' asked the young Turk

'He is Frankish,' replied the guard.

'Yaranqash?'

So Rigaud became Yaranqash. Worse was to follow. As was the custom with many slaves, especially those to be entrusted with serving within the close circle of a powerful ruler's court, Rigaud or Yaranqash as he was now called, was castrated. In a world where assassination was commonplace, it was thought that such men would no longer be a threat to the safety of their master. Rigaud had no sooner felt that he deserved to be called a man than he had it most cruelly taken from him. He had become

Yaranqash, the eunuch. He never forgave those who did it though, in the years afterwards as he served Zengi, none would have known the hatred he held in his heart.

Zengi became the atabeg of Mosul at the age of thirty two and then of Aleppo a year later. At his formal investiture by the Sultan, the tribes of the region brought gifts of horses, slaves, precious stones, gold ornaments, ivories and even exotic animals. At his master's side, as always, was his faithful retainer, Yaranqash.

One old sheikh from a poor tribe of the arid desert, apologising for the quality of his gifts, produced a strange item in a box of sandal wood.

'Perhaps it will amuse your excellency. We think it is from a time even before the Patriarchs, even before the Great Flood.'

Zengi took the strangely shaped skull from its box and after a cursory examination tossed it to Yaranqash. The slave caught it and looked into the blank eye sockets. Immediately, he felt his mind swimming with images, overlapping and dissolving one into another. He felt a tremor run through him and his pulse and breathing quickened. Something deep in his genes was being stirred, the ghostly outlines of a long lost lineage trapped in his nerve ends were feeling the pull of the skull.

Zengi was a skilled warrior, tactician and when needs be, a bargainer and forger of alliances. He was an astute judge of men and quick to notice the change in his servant as he handled the skull. It intrigued him and, thanking the old sheikh for his gift, he dismissed the court and met privately with Yaranqash.

'What is it about this skull that you feel when you hold it? I felt nothing but I saw you did.'

'I'm not sure, your Excellency, but it was as though I could glimpse into the thoughts of those bringing gifts. It was not clear. Much was mixed up and confused.'

'You could read their minds?'

'No. Not quite. Just... little bits… Ideas.'

Zengi immediately saw the advantages of his slave's newly acquired ability

'You must practice. From now on you will sit by me at every meeting and use the skull. Probe their minds. Tell me what they think, what they plan.'

From that time on Yaranqash sat with his hands on the dome of the skull all concealed beneath a silk drape and tried to capture the thoughts or, at least the mood, of everyone with whom his master did business.

Zengi formed alliances, made and broke treaties, attacked Turks and Crusaders alike, all in his pursuit of power and at every step, every parley or truce, every bargain or deal, he was accompanied by his silent body servant, his fair hair bleached blonde by the desert sun, sitting to one side, cross-legged, his hands hidden under the purple silk draped over is knees, watching the faces of all present. So insignificant did he seem that no-one noticed him nor remarked on the fact that the slave remained seated even in the presence of Zengi himself and the visiting emirs and commanders with whom he dealt.

In the private chambers, Yaranqash would recount to his master the images, the impressions he had received from those present and enable the atabeg to pre-empt his enemies and to attack or retreat when circumstances favoured him, always taking him closer to his ultimate goal of Damascus, the Pearl of the Desert. The prize of the great cosmopolitan city, its green oasis surrounded by the desert sands, was what drove Zengi on.

He defended the city in an alliance with its ruler against the Crusaders, besieged the city himself and failing to take it, he retreated and made peace. He fought with and against Crusaders, Byzantines, Damascenes and other Seljuks in a series of alliances and combinations, always with the conquest of Damascus in mind and always with his servant Yaranqash at his side.

In the harem of the atabeg was a young girl, captured at Baalbek and destined to become one of the concubines. Yaranqash saw in her all the grace and beauty he could wish for in a woman. She smiled as she passed, and his heart was taken. She made him aware as he had not been for many years of the great wrong that had been done to him. True, he had a position of trust in the innermost circle of a feared and successful warrior with access to riches and power had he wished it, but he had not, nor ever could have, the love of any woman in the truest sense. The rage and resentment boiled in him as he watched his master's regular demands to his harem for women to his bed, especially if it was for the girl from Baalbek.

His festering hatred grew and grew though years of servitude had schooled him in hiding any feelings he might have. One night, as Zengi slept, the pent up dam of hatred burst and Yaranqash stabbed the atabeg over and over again. Stepping back from the bleeding corpse, he realised what he had done and fled for his life. Many could have stopped him but their master had been a cruel and violent man who had flayed and crucified on a whim and few were sorry at his fate. Carrying the skull, the eunuch fled to Damascus, to Zengi's enemy, the governor, Mu'in ad Din, hoping for sanctuary.

Poor Yaranqash, despite the effect he could elicit from the skull, he little understood the politics of the Turkish world. His years as a confidante of Zengi had made him forget how he would be viewed by another ruler. He was a slave who had betrayed his master. His only use was as a bargaining chip in the game of politics between warring factions. He was dispatched to Zengi's sons who had him executed. He refused to disclose the effect of the skull hoping the secret might buy him time but Mu'in ad-Din, had seen silver encased skulls before as war trophies and it meant nothing to him. He thought it might make an amusing present.

Always suspicious of Zengi's sons, the governor of Damascus concluded a truce with the Crusader, King Baldwin of Jerusalem, allowing him room to manoeuvre against his Turkic enemies. Among the caravan of gifts sent to the Christian ruler of the Holy City was a sandalwood box containing a strangely shaped, silver mounted skull.

The box sat in the treasury of the Kings of Jerusalem, a minor tribute of no significance until the leprous Baldwin IV found reason to reward his loyal Templars.

Saladin from his power base in Egypt, had replaced the Turkic rulers of Syria as the main threat to the Crusader kingdoms.

Odo de Armand was Marshal of Jerusalem and Grand Master of the The Poor Knights of the Temple of Solomon - the Templars. He was a headstrong but inspiring military leader. As Saladin's army marched to attack the city, King Baldwin IV called upon the knights to support his defence of his realm. At Montsigard, in true Templar fashion, with no regard to personal safety, they engaged the ranks of the superior Muslim force in a thunderous charge, smashing through and creating disorder and panic. This was a classic Templar tactic, the sheer impetus of the heavy cavalry like a shock wave, breaking the enemy's line and allowing their supporting troops to pour into the breach. Saladin had to retreat and, for now, the Holy City was secure under Crusader rule.

In the aftermath, Baldwin approached Odo.

'I wish to reward you for your courage and leadership which, I am sure, won us the day.'

'As our name suggests, we are monks with vows of poverty and seek no reward other than that of divine grace.'

'Nevertheless, while in no way wishing to place a burden on your avowed state, I have something which I feel the order may have as a trophy of the battle. This came to my uncle after the saving of Damascus, how appropriate it should come to you after the saving of the greater jewel of Jerusalem. It is of no value so it doesn't break your vow of poverty, but it allows me to express my gratitude.'

He clapped his hands and a servant scurried forward carrying the sandalwood box. Odo accepted the gift, insisting he did so on behalf of the order, not himself.

Odo felt he owed no fealty to the king. He was, after all, Marshal of Jerusalem, and Grand Master of the Knights Templar. By Papal Bull, the only power over the Templars was the Pope in Rome, however, he accepted the gift with due courtesy and withdrew to his chambers with a degree of curiosity. What was it that was deemed to have no value yet had been given as a gift to kings?

In the sparsely furnished room befitting a warrior-monk, he opened the box and regarded the contents with puzzlement. A skull; mounted with silver and appearing to be oddly shaped but otherwise unremarkable. Skulls were sent as war trophies on occasions but usually those of noted enemies and this one appeared to be extremely old, almost like stone in its appearance. Was there significance in the choice of this gift or did the monarch simply want rid of it?

He lifted the skull from its box and held it up, the empty eye sockets looking at him. As he stared into them, he felt his head swim and a strange aura surrounded him. He felt he could hear voices but not catch the words, sensations of taste and smell, and a feeling of detachment from the world.

Unnerved, he returned the skull to its resting place and sat down, feeling the strange effects subside. He contemplated the box and its contents. He was a knight, trained in the art of warfare, fearless in the face of armed enemies. He was from a long line of warriors. His people had dwelt in Limousin in the Pais d'Oc from time immemorial and defended their land against all invaders. His Gaulish ancestors had fought against Julius Caesar in the Gallic Wars. What he did not know, could not know, was that the blood of an even older race had left its traces in him, a race whose burial places lay hidden beneath his native soil.

Odo had never flinched in battle and he was not about to retreat from this unknown assault on his senses. He picked up the skull and focussed his mind on the almost hallucinatory effects, trying to pin down the shifting visions and sounds. He began to get hints of past thoughts as if in the mind of others but who or where they were, he could not judge. He was not sure what the skull could do for or to him. At first he thought it might be some devilry employed by Baldwin for his own purposes, but he recognised that the king, though brave and stoical was not one for whom esoteric arts would hold any interest. The knight concluded that the gift had been given in the manner the king had stated, a simple trophy of one battle given in victory at another. King Baldwin had had no idea of the latent power of the skull. Perhaps he had never held it or, if he had, he lacked the ability to release it.

Odo made several further attempts to master the effects of holding the skull and, eventually, he was able to realise its potential though he could never quite hold on to the tantalising glimpses his mind was shown. As a devout member of a religious order, he prayed long and hard for guidance. Was this a tool of the devil or was it a legitimate tool in the fight to preserve the Holy Land for Christianity? To the knight, the answer was straightforward. A sword or a lance could be used for good or evil, it simply depended on who was using it and for what purpose. If the skull could aid the Crusaders' cause then it, like his sword, was being used in a noble cause and so could not be the work of the Devil. Having settled the matter in his own mind, he summoned his senior knights to disclose the matter to them. All were sworn to the utmost secrecy.

Each, in turn, handled the skull and reported their reactions. Most felt nothing but a young man called Gerard with sandy fair hair who had only recently joined the knights in the service of King Baldwin, felt the force of the talisman. With eyes downcast and head bowed, he mumbled that he had received what he called visions but would say no more. Later, in private, he disclosed to Odo that he had indeed been privy to the innermost feelings and thoughts of some in the room, their doubts and misgivings, their concern that this might be some trick of Satan but also of their utter loyalty and devotion to their order and their vow of secrecy.

Later, Odo would use Gerard's ability to read the thoughts of others but was not forewarned of his own capture and death in Saladin's prison. Seeing beyond the veil of time was not a gift given even to those who had some mastery of the skull's potential. Gerard could not save the Master.

When Gerard de Ridefort eventually rose to become Grand Master, the skull would aid his political manoeuvrings with the kings and dukes of the Outremer as the Crusader states were known; the rival Hospitaller knights; Saladin and the Muslim forces; the Holy See of Rome and the European monarchies. Balancing the demands and needs of one group against the threats and advances of another alongside the neutralisation of a third was greatly assisted by the ability to gauge the real intentions of the negotiators.

For five years, he trod a fine line accumulating wealth and success to the order until his judgement failed at the siege of Templar fortress of Acre and, despite his ability to access the powers of the skull, he suffered the fate of his predecessor.

Even in the days of The Watcher, it had been given to only a few to see beyond the thoughts of others and to glimpse the future. This was not to happen to the order for decades to come.

The skull continued to be presented at the initiation of new knights to check on the possibility of a response, but these were rare and feeble. This ritual was to have the unfortunate consequence that the uninitiated heard fragments of the proceedings and the Templars were rumoured to be blasphemously worshipping an idol, a head, and to indulge in sacrilegious practices. This accusation would come to haunt them and help bring them down.

CHAPTER 9

For generations, the Crusader kingdoms of the Holy Land continued to exist in the shifting sands of alliances and truces, sieges and skirmishes, of battles and campaigns, assassinations and annexations, of Turks and Seljuks, Christians and Moslems, Europeans and Arabs. Rulers arose and were deposed, kings and governors, sultans and emirs came and went.

Eventually, the tide turned. The states created by the Crusaders collapsed and the Templars were driven from the Near East to Cyprus and back to Europe.

Jacques de Molay had been a young knight in the time of Grand Masters Odo and Gerard when the Templars were a force across the Levant. He too had held the skull and learned to use its power but Jacques had experienced something none of the others had felt. He had glimpsed the future. Not realising that the shadowy visions that crept half-formed into his brain were actual events to come, as a devout believer he thought they were warnings from God to his favoured warrior-monks in order that they might avert the disasters foretold.

Fearing the worst when trying to resurrect the fortunes of the bearded brethren, he ordered that much of the Templars' wealth be distributed to secret locations where sympathetic followers would guard it for the revival that he hoped for and for the next Crusade. The account books were destroyed and every member of the order was expressly forbidden to speak of any of their rituals. The secret of the skull was to be preserved.

Calling on his two most trusted men who had served alongside him since the fall of the Crusader citadel at Acre, he ordered that the skull be taken in secret far from the reaches of those whom he now recognised as enemies of the Order, Philip, king of France and the new Pope, Clement. The knights were instructed to carry the skull to where the writ of neither monarch nor pope was effective.

Too late, when he was captured, tortured and condemned to be burned alive as a heretic, did Molay come to realise that the images he had seen when he held the skull were not a divine warning but a prophecy. One of the charges levelled against him and his fellow Templars was that they had committed sacrilege by worshipping a severed head.

The skull had been unable to save them, and a twisted rumour of its existence had added to their alleged crimes.

A residue of its latent power still lay in Molay's brain when, under the excruciating pain of his death throes, he saw the future clear and stark. He shouted out his prediction of the death of Philip and Pope Clement within the year and the untimely deaths of all Philip's descendants causing the fall of his royal house, the end of the Capet dynasty.

Jacques de Molay became a legend in the flames in front of Notre Dame having shared for a brief moment in his final agonies, a sight of the future. The gift of the Watcher.

The skull was already on its way to safety and secrecy.

CHAPTER 10

A day off and a chance to start the long delayed search for the Arrow Stone. The delay was in large part due to his own procrastination. He knew it might well be a tedious chore, but its existence nagged at the back of his mind. He really would like to find it.

The last record of its whereabouts had mentioned it being re-used in a wall somewhere in the area northwest of St Abbs Head. The area included the lands of Northfield. Northfield had once been a small village, a ferm-toun in the old Scots tongue, then it had given its name to a barony with extensive lands extending right up on to the surrounding moors and heights where sea eagles had soared and choughs had tumbled. Now they were gone, and the barony divided into several farms covering hundreds of acres, including a nature reserve. Bounded by the huge cliffs like those at Fast Castle and the massif of St Abbs Head where the Lammermuirs finally dipped their toes into the grey waters of the North Sea, it had miles of drystone dykes to search and since the Arrow Stone was carved only on one side, it would mean scanning both sides of the dykes, twice the distance to walk.

Still, he thought, trying to make light of his self-imposed chore, the scenery is beautiful, the bird life fascinating and, if the weather holds, it's a better way to keep fit than pounding away in some sweaty gym.

He gave himself some mental instructions. I have to be systematic. Mobile signal is unreliable so can't always get a GPS fix. Get a map, follow each field boundary and cross it off when done rather than just wander from place to place. So, equipped with a 1:25000 O.S. map, he set off.

Initially, he thought the fact that many of the old dykes had been replaced by fencing would make his task easier then he realised, although the dykes had gone, many of the stones still remained along the field margins. He would have to check each one. He might strike lucky and if he didn't find it, so what. There were plenty other petroglyphs to chase up. With that insouciant thought, he strode down the road to the lighthouse and started on the nearest dyke.

He was scanning the finely balanced interlinked pattern of boulders that made up the wall when he caught sight of a vaguely familiar tweedy figure striding down the narrow roadway. It was the inquiring member from his recent tour group. The one that reminded him of an old school mistress.

'Hello, I remember you from the trip. I didn't realise you were spending some time here.'

She regarded him with a look as if to dismiss his impertinence, then seemed to decide against it and was almost friendly.

'Spur of the moment decision.'

She half turned to go then turned back with a trace of a smile.

'Perhaps I was inspired by your informative lectures.'

As she strode off, he wondered if there was a hint of humour in the line. He gave a wry little grin to himself and returned to his task.

CHAPTER 11

The times were changing. The Bruce was dead, thirteen years after his conclusive victory at Bannockburn. He had died as the recognised King of Scots with his excommunication removed. His son and heir to the throne was a five year old boy, King David II. In return for recognition of his father's sovereignty, David had been married at the age of four to the sister of Edward, the English king. The Plantagenet king still had designs on his northern neighbour and took advantage of the weakness of the Bruce dynasty to support rival claimants in a series of encounters that ended badly for the Scots. The young king and his bride were sent to France for safety. At the same time, Jacques de Molay's curse, his glimpse of the future, was unfolding as the descendants of Philip, the accursed kings, would witness the house of Capet fall from power.

Brother Gilbert heard word of the political manoeuvrings of the great and powerful. It was more than twenty years since he and his fellow knight had landed on the coast with their burden. They had cast off the white surcoat with the scarlet cross and assumed the black robes of the Benedictines. His companion had gone, dying in one of the periodic epidemics of fever and pestilence that swept through the land, reminding the fearful peasants of God's wrath at their sins.

His sword had rested in the locked chest in his cell as he took up the hoe and spade to tend the Priory gardens. He kept himself apart from the other monks even at times when conversation was allowed, and he still wore his beard. He was, and would always be, a member of the Poor Fellow-Soldiers of Christ and of the Temple of Solomon; a Templar. He had guarded the secret with which he had been entrusted, the secret that now only he knew existed.

With some disquiet he heard the news of the defeat of the Scottish armies at Halidon Hill, a mere twelve miles away and the flight of the Scottish child king to France to the protection of the French king, the king that was the heir of Philip, the destroyer of his beloved order. The refuge was no longer secure. He resolved to act.

The new prior had been seriously injured in a fall from his horse while returning from Lindisfarne and the priory was being administered from Durham. The strength of papal influence now that Scotland's royal family were no longer excommunicants was another concern for the old Templar. Gilbert took advantage of the administrative confusion to retrieve the sandal wood box, unopened since it left the hands of Jacques de Molay, from the locked chest in his cell. Monks were not supposed to have personal possessions but, on arrival, he had made it clear that the chest was to be kept in his small room and no-one had ever queried it. Most had almost forgotten its existence and some of the younger monks were not even aware of it.

Saddling a horse, he rode up on to the high moor and made for the castle where he had landed by the light of a flaming brazier those many years before. His destination wasn't the keep. It had been occupied by English levies after the defeat of Halidon Hill. Crossing the marshy moorland by the old route through the peat workings kept him out of sight of any sentries on the battlements and let him leave his steed in the steep dean leading to the shoreline below the towering cliffs.

Now on foot, he picked his way down a path between cliff and sea to where a series of caves pierced the foot of the sheer rock face. One in particular looked uninviting to the casual observer, a narrow triangular cleft that just allowed a man of his size to squeeze in by lying on his side. He had explored it many years before and knew it was roomier once he passed the stricture of the entrance, but it certainly wasn't one that anyone would choose to enter. Crawling and shuffling along the passage, he reached the far end and then reached up. In the dark, he could feel his way upwards into a second cave only accessible through a hole in the roof. Once into the upper chamber, he felt secure enough to strike tinder and light a candle. He had shed his woollen cloak at the entrance and under his habit he had wrapped round his body layers of cerecloth used by the monks as shrouds for the dead. Impregnated with a mixture of beeswax and linseed oil, it would make a waterproof covering for the box. Having wrapped it carefully, he knelt and said a prayer for those who had suffered in its keeping, then, easing the package into a leather bag, he snuffed out the candle, dropped into the lower chamber and crawled backwards out of the cave.

Outside, he checked that his reappearance had not been noted and climbed back up to his horse. On the cliff top, he committed to memory various obvious and permanent landmarks that would allow the exact position of the cave to be located. Looking up at the night sky he noted the stars of the Great Bear and from this, the position of the Pole Star, due north.

Leading his steed, he returned to his route then rode back across the moor to the priory.

Very early the next day, with the marks still fresh in his mind, he sought out the piles of quarried stone that the masons were using to extend the refectory and, choosing a squared and dressed block, he set to work with chisel and mallet to create a map of the site of the cave.

An incised line across the stone represented the coastline and another double groove, the road to the castle. Spirals represented prominent hills and circles, the offshore rocks. A deep cup stood for the cave and over it he carved the Templar cross. To one side, he cut an arrow shape pointing to a tiny star mark – Polaris. This would allow the stone to be oriented correctly at any future date.

He had seen the cup and ring markings that were to be to be found all over the area and had no doubt his stone would be considered another of the same, quarried from some outcrop and carted to the Priory for the masons' use. He rubbed earth into the chisel marks to age them and place the stone to one side of the pile.

Later, he returned as the workmen were starting their day and engaged them in conversation, though his mastery of the local dialect was limited. He expressed admiration for their work and commiserated with them about their wages and conditions of employment. He took an interest in their skill as craftsmen and casually pointed out the block of stone remarking how much better was their ability to produce carving than the primitive pagan wretch who had obviously created the cup and ring marked stone.

'Still, it would be fitting that such a stone would be put to use building the house of God. Saint Augustine did say that we should not destroy the pagan temples but sanctify them for use by the Holy Church. Perhaps it would make a lintel for the door to the refectory.'

Having implanted this suggestion in the master mason's mind where he knew it would be regarded as an instruction, he blessed the men and returned to the daily round of priory life.

In the evening, after compline when his companions had retired for the day, he slipped unnoticed into the scriptorium where the manuscripts were copied and, taking parchment and ink, composed a letter to William Sinclair, Bishop of Dunkeld who, with Templar support, had led the charge of cavalry to defeat an English army landing on the Fife coast in Bruce's war. Sinclair had always been sympathetic to the order. Within what seemed to be a simple report of his life and work since his arrival at Coldingham Priory and giving the news of the death of his erstwhile companion from a fever some years before Gilbert managed, by means of some ciphers used by the Order, to conceal the details of what had become of the box and its contents. He indicated where the map could be found, innocently and permanently integrated into the fabric of the ecclesiastical house that had given them sanctuary.

The structure of the Templars had been destroyed. There was no longer a Grand Master, no Seneschal, no commanders, not even knights and sergeants. They were now all monks.

He felt that someone with the power and position of the Bishop of Dunkeld would know what to do with the secret of the sandalwood box.

What Gilbert didn't know and would never know was that, in the confusion of civil war, rebellion, usurpation between royalists and claimants, opportunists and loyalists, Bishop

William had changed his allegiance. The letter carried through the channels of Templar supporters never reached him and, after a time, vanished into obscurity.

The warrior-monk knew age was catching up with him. Old wounds ached and he found the work tiring now. The damp sea mists and the bitter winter winds made him long for the fierce sun of the Holy Land where he had soldiered in the name of the Church. He felt that they had failed there but still had faith that they might be resurgent under a new Grand Master and once more regain the Holy City. He had done his best. He had saved the skull for the Order and the future. He felt relieved of his burden and able to live out his days far from his native land, an end he could never have imagined when he had gone to do battle with the Turks all those years ago.

CHAPTER 12

David was searching along the line of a wall having fruitlessly criss-crossed the fields of St Abbs Head on every day he had had off from his tourist guide role in the past month.

The area was a black spot for mobile phone reception so his initial intention to try to use GPS navigation had to be abandoned and he had fallen back on the skills of the Ordnance Survey teams and their detailed maps.

His next tour would be his last for the season so, though his income would be seriously curtailed, he would have more time for his task. He had toyed with the idea of asking Kate out for a meal, a bottle of wine perhaps. The area was a bit of a gastronomic desert though the use of the Discovery gave him a bit more scope. Initially, he'd thought to invite her to dinner at his cottage and show off his newly acquired culinary skills but then decided that a neutral venue would be better for a first. A first what? A first date? He still found Kate a bit confusing.

He was musing on this vein when he caught sight of the kayak with its drysuited occupant down below at the old fishing station of Pettico Wick. Used by the sub-aqua enthusiasts that thronged to the area every summer, drawn by the clear waters close the Head and the extensive sea life in the Marine Reserve, the old pier allowed for the launching of inflatables and easy access to the water. He waved enthusiastically, almost manically, and eventually caught Kate's eye. She waved back and gestured to him to come down.

'Hello there. How's the search going?'

'Not at all. No luck. Nothing that even looks like a carved stone.'

'I suppose that's better than getting your hopes up only to be disappointed.'

'I wouldn't mind just the occasional rise in the pulse rate. Just to break the monotony.'

'Oh well, if it's pulses racing you're looking for, we'll have to see what can be done about that.'

'Eh?'

He was taken aback by what seemed to be her rather suggestive remark

Kate grinned at his discomfiture. She liked his somewhat gauche manner and had a schoolgirl urge to tease him. He did remind her of an earlier time in her life when relationships had been more fun. The so-called research post had been a convenient way out of a relationship within the university department. She had come to realise he (he was now just "he" in her mind, she couldn't bring herself to think, let alone say, his name) wasn't going to jeopardise his career and his family for her despite any rash promises he may have made.

The bird counting job had come up and he had been only too happy to agree to a secondment from the department though she had made sure that her pay and grading were not compromised. She had got tough and a little cynical.

David's charm was that he was so unlike the men she had known in recent years, the calculating, honours-seeking career scientists, the ones who always insisted that their name appeared on any research paper that has been produced from their department even if their input had been minimal. She found his enthusiasm for his petroglyphs and his concern in giving his elderly adventurers in bus seats an experience to remember, refreshing and endearing. She resolved to resist the temptation to tease him.

'Seriously, if you could give me some idea of what this stone looks like, I could help.'

'You would? That would be marvellous, but what about your bird census stuff.'

'Well, not all days are suitable for counting and I would like to spin the job out a little.'

She didn't mention why.

'Two eyes are better than one or, better still, four eyes are better than two.'

He laughed.

'Great. You're on. Here, I'll give you my mobile number, but I warn you, half the time you won't get a signal here especially if you're down at the shore. Phone me when you've got some time off and, if it fits with my time off, we've got a date.

He finished shyly.

Kate resisted the temptation to tease.

'That we will have.'

David decide to seize the opportunity.

'Would you like to come out for a meal one evening? There's not a great choice around here but there are some reasonable eateries.'

Kate looked at him and saw the genuine friendship in his face.

'I'd love to.'

'Tomorrow?'

He felt he might be pushing it a bit and was relieved to hear her say

'Yes. That sounds just fine but I insist equal shares. No silly male gallantry stuff.'

'Right-oh. I'll pick you up at about eight. That okay?'

She nodded and he turned to climb the steps up from the old pier.

'See you then.'

'See you.'

He almost bounded up the steps and halfway up, he waved back down as she paddled her kayak back out into the cove. She didn't see the gesture but thought to herself that it was nice to feel like a teenager again.

CHAPTER 13

For forty years Auguste Daubin had been a dealer in antique books and manuscripts. Sometimes, if he thought it would improve the chance of a sale or to improve the provenance of a nondescript tome, he was Auguste D'Aubin with a line about access to penniless aristocrats having to sell off the family libraries. From grimoires and alchemical treatises to parchments and papyri, French or English, Latin or Greek, Arabic or Hebrew, he could tell a forgery within minutes. Equally, he could sense the genuine article.

When a bundle of leatherbound books of religious studies, some with gold tooling and stamped covers came across his desk, he knew this was a marketable commodity. Unlike some of Auguste's sales, they had truly been part of an extensive library that had been broken up to pay death taxes. Gathered from all the European cities by a bibliophile duke, many of his treasures had stood in serried ranks on the shelves of his bookcases for generations while his descendants had concerned themselves with the less cerebral activities that had ultimately led to the impoverishment of the once great family and the need to dispose of its treasures. Paintings, furniture and all the vast library had been catalogued and auctioned. This bundle had been sold as "14th/15th century, Scottish".

Books, especially ancient books had value. They were collectable. Rich men bought books for the same reasons they bought art or stamps or gold coins. They were purchased as a safeguard, as a hedge against the vagaries of the market or currency fluctuations. There were a few true bibliophiles or art lovers who truly valued these objects for what they were but for most they provided a supplement to existing fortunes and a means of demonstrating the wealth and culture of an individual. Beautiful books were supposed to speak volumes about their owner even if they had only been given a cursory glance after their purchase. A commodity that, if one was in difficult financial straits, could be converted to cash.

Thus, it was that a small bundle of obscure volumes bound with a faded ribbon had come up for auction. It had been bought on spec by a dealer who had identified it as having the potential for a quick mark-up and sell-on to Monsieur Daubin, as someone who would be more likely to find a specific client. Such was the antique trade. No-one actually sat and looked at the items for their own sake. No-one actually read the books. No-one, that is, until they came to Auguste.

As he inspected the items, he noticed a single document between the leaves of one of the books, possibly used as a book mark or perhaps deliberately hidden from view. The dealer was distractedly looking at some prints on the office wall and hadn't noticed so Auguste quickly closed the covers and thought of the parchment as a bonus. Manuscripts had a resale value of their own. A price was agreed, the dealer left and Auguste, on his own, in that tiny cluttered office, became the first person in five centuries to view Gilbert's missive.

The simple wax seal lacked any insignia and had been carefully opened probably with a hot knife but from the folds of the document and the condition of the wax, it looked as though it had been opened once then an attempt had been made to reseal it. Couched in poor Latin with odd words in what appeared to be French or Provençal, the contents were barely understandable.

Auguste managed to decipher enough to see that the words did not refer to any momentous historic event but appeared to be an account of simple monastic life. The hand was clumsy, certainly not that of a trained scribe.

The old book seller was feeling somewhat disappointed with his purchase when he noticed, between the lines of script, strange little geometric shapes, fainter than the written words and drawn with a finer implement.

A cipher. His pulse quickened. Ciphers were good business. There was always a good market for documents with secret messages and he knew just the man who might pay for such a find.

No-one could know the entire market, but one could know the dealers who would know the specialists who would have interested private clients. Each would have their percentage and the price would rise with each link in the chain, but this was not important for the final sale would be to someone who didn't need to ask the price.

Pierre Gabrin considered himself a citizen of the world. His Maronite ancestors had welcomed the Christian knights of the First Crusade and had been present at the last withdrawal from the Levant to Cyprus when Saladin asserted his sovereignty over Jerusalem. From Cyprus to France, the diaspora had spread to the Americas. Successive generations of entrepreneurs with a strong sense of family had made Pierre extremely, if discreetly, wealthy. He was able to indulge his passions which included the history of the lands of his forefathers. He had read every book, treatise and dissertation he could find from the Phoenicians and Canaanites to the Ottomans and the French. He had a particular interest in the Crusader kingdoms. He had found that Arabic sources painted a different picture to that of European histories and often contained details overlooked in other writings. The description of the Templars was quite different from the stereotyped images so familiar in European literature.

They appeared to have embraced much of the culture of the land they sought to hold for

Christendom. Many aspects of the east had rubbed off on these warrior-monks. Some, it seemed, had developed an interest in mysticism, others had dabbled in mind altering substances. There were references to fugues and visionary episodes and, just occasionally, a mention of cult objects as a means of achieving these states. The word "skull" occurred in the older texts but was usually regarded as a mistranslation for "head". Pierre collected texts from any source that might have a bearing on his obsession. He was a regular client of Monsieur Daubin.

'My dear Auguste, it's been so long since we last met. How are you?'

'As ever. I get older.' He shrugged.

'Yes, none of us escapes the years. I got your message. You have something for me?'

'Indeed. Not exactly your usual but when I saw it, I immediately thought this will interest the estimable Pierre Gabrin.'

The pair smiled after this exchange of pleasantries, two old friends sharing an understanding.

'Well then, what is it?'

Auguste was enjoying his moment and wouldn't be hurried.

'A rare item. A very unusual item. I don't think I've come across anything quite like it before.'

'Auguste. Less of your nonsense. Let me see this marvel.'

The bookseller pushed the letter across the desk. His client picked up a magnifying glass and looked closely at the document.

'Why is this of interest to me? It appears to be a fairly banal letter in poor Latin, and it addresses a Bishop of Dunkeld. Where is Dunkeld and why should I be interested in him?'

Auguste leaned over.

'But see. Between the upstrokes of the letters. See the cryptograms. This letter contains a message.'

Pierre looked again

'Yes, and you're sure it's the genuine article?'

Auguste looked pained

'Pierre, old friend. Have I ever let you down?'

'No, no. Of course not. Have you any idea about the message?'

'No. but I was sure you, with all your...'

He didn't like to say "money".

'…your wide circle of acquaintances. You will know where to find the answer'

Gabrin looked into the distance, a slight furrow across his brow then a slow smile twitched from his lips.

'Yes, I think I do.'

'I knew you couldn't resist a secret. A puzzle, even if it isn't in your usual line.'

A price was agreed, and the bookseller carefully eased the parchment into a protective folder as Pierre signed the cheque.

'You'll let me know if the message leads you to a secret treasure,' he joked.

'But, of course, old friend.'

As Pierre stood up to take his leave, Auguste motioned to the folder.

'By the way, Dunkeld is in Scotland but that was *to* where the letter was sent. More interesting would be *from* where and *from* whom it was sent and why they used a cipher. What information was so important that it had to be hidden?'

Pierre paused and thought.

'Thanks. I'll keep in touch.'

With a nod of friendship and thanks, the businessman left, the folder tucked into the inside pocket of his well-cut jacket.

As the dealer had said, Pierre did have a large number of acquaintances, not friends but acquaintances with whom he was friendly. He was of a slightly self-effacing nature with a natural interest in others. He preferred that others spoke about themselves than asked about him and, as most people liked to speak about themselves, he was regarded as agreeable company. Thus, he had a wide circle of contacts mostly, but not exclusively, of a business nature.

He was due to fly to New York on business and decided to travel on to Washington to look up one such contact who just might have the means to access the message of the strange cryptograms. He made a copy of them to avoid having to carry the parchment around and also to keep their origin hidden. He scanned the original document and, for the same reason, removed the cryptograms from the copy. He felt that the sender had intended that the letter and its message should be viewed separately and so they should be investigated separately. He then emailed a name from the past and, saying he was to be in Washington D.C. for a few days, suggesting a meeting for a drink or a meal to catch up with one another.

CHAPTER 14

Brett Steiger worked for a department of the government of the United States. He never fully disclosed where in the governmental structure he fitted, laughing off specific enquiries.

'You wouldn't have heard of us. Mostly admin stuff. All about contracts and meeting various specifications and rules about government funding. All *very* boring, but, you know, someone has to do it, and it pays the rent.'

What he omitted to explain was that the contracts were mostly for work done on behalf of the U.S. government in places such as the Middle East many of which were of a "sensitive" nature.

Pierre Gabrin with his extensive networks in the area from Lebanon to the Gulf had been extremely useful to Steiger and, as a quid pro quo, Steiger had helped him to secure business deals for his companies. Steiger liked the guy. He was good company and not too pushy, always remembering the names of his wife and daughters and, over the years, providing them with small but amusing gifts that had raised Steiger's own standing with his hypercritical teenagers. It had been a long time since they had met. Both were now somewhat removed from the front line of intelligence. Steiger was now "back office" and Gabrin was quietly pursuing his many business interests.

He also had no illusions about Pierre Gabrin and knew he was a shrewd if charming entrepreneur with an eye for any chance that might come along and wouldn't be too fussy about the legality or morality of any transaction.

I wonder what he wants, he thought.

Still, it would be a welcome break from the tedium of intelligence gathering and the murkier side of international politics. He looked forward to an evening with a slightly more unconventional companion than the squash playing, career-minded young people who staffed his department and whose energy and commitment made him feel old.

CHAPTER 15

David arrived promptly at the rented cottage with the Discovery. At the door, Kate glanced over his shoulder.

'That looks a bit more comfortable than my wee car.'

She was ready and he noticed she had definitely made an effort. Gone was the hair-tied-back, field scientist look to be replaced by a much softer image. He thought she looked truly beautiful.

'You look lovely,' he blurted out.

'Why, thank you, Sir,' she replied with a gracious nod. 'You've scrubbed up quite well yourself.'

He held open the passenger door for her and she gave a playful mock curtsey before climbing in.

'We're going to a nice little inn, a few miles away. Doesn't look much but the food's good'

'Great. I'm famished. Drive on!'

The evening was a success. The chef excelled himself. The menu was from genuine local produce not pub grub out of the back of a van and the ambience in the old inn was relaxed and friendly. David was well aware of the stringent Scottish laws on drinking and driving but thought one glass of wine was permissible and he raised the glass in a toast.

'Here's to your kayak on the roof rack, without which tonight wouldn't have happened.'

Kate laughed and raised her glass.

'Yes. Here's to the kayak.'

The rest of the meal was spent exchanging information about themselves and their backgrounds. David admitted that he hadn't done much since leaving university, travelled a bit, taken odd jobs. His travels had inevitably brought him to petroglyph sites.

'I suppose I will end up teaching,' he said.

'There's nothing dead end about teaching,' replied Kate. 'Good teachers are the most valuable members of society. Ask anyone who their favourite teacher was, and you'll get an instant answer. Everyone remembers the good teacher.'

'And the awful ones. I wouldn't want to be the one they all laughed about or hated.'

'You wouldn't be. You're an enthusiast and however kids try to hide it and be cool, they do respond to that.'

'Yourself? What's after the bird counting?'

'Oh, I don't know'

She became slightly guarded as the question called up some decisions she had been avoiding.

'I should go back and finish my thesis, I suppose. This is just a secondment, a break.'

She quickly changed the subject.

'Tell me about the Arrow Stone. What does it look like? I can't help you look for it if I don't know what to look for.'

'Well. Neither do I, really. There are no drawings of it and the references just say it has an arrow carved on it as well as the cup and ring marks. It was used as a door lintel originally so it must be quite sizeable but to be honest, I don't know if it even exists any more. The last reference to it was over fifty years ago. All I have to go on is a mention of a wall to the land northwest of St Abbs head.'

'In return for your taking me for this excellent meal, I will do at least one day's searching for your stone. Mind you I'm still going halfers on the meal.'

When they arrived back at the cottage she spared him the decision making again as she leaned across and kissed him.

'Thanks for the evening.'

A pause.

'We must do it again,' he said, hopefully.

'Yes. I'd like that. I'll give you a call when I'm free. To seek the stone.'

She made it sound like a line from Tolkien.

'Goodnight.'

He drove home in high spirits. Things were looking decidedly hopeful.

CHAPTER 16

Brett Steiger and Pierre Gabrin were reminiscing over old times and old contacts, over episodes that never made it into official reports, over times when both had been younger and less risk-averse. Pierre had recalled when certain coded messages had found their way to Brett with advantageous results.

What's he up to? What's this leading to? thought Steiger.

'Oddly enough, I have a piece of coding that I came across in an old manuscript, fourteenth century. An old letter and it intrigued me. It's probably nothing. Maybe a message that was once of significance but only a historical curio now. Probably of no importance but, you know how things get to one. A loose end as it were. I'd like to find out what it's all about. You know how I never liked loose ends.'

He passed the copied cryptogram across to Steiger who studied it carefully.

'So that's it. Just a piece of code? No background. No indication who was meant to read it?'

'Well, it was in a letter from a monk to a bishop. In Scotland.'

'I might be able to help. I know some guys who specialise in this sorta stuff. I'll tell them it is for some historical research to do with... something Scottish. The Stone of Destiny!'

Pierre laughed.

'I am most grateful. I know it's just a whim, but I'd like to sort it out. As I said, I hate loose ends.'

The two men shook hands and Gabrin left.

Steiger sat down. Loose ends, my ass, he thought. What's that wily old stoat up to? He resolved to get the cryptanalysts to run the code through their programs. It looked fairly simple. He would spin them some story about why it was needed but keep the details of his chat with Gabrin to himself for the time being. He didn't give another thought to his flippant reference to the Stone of Destiny.

Steiger's contact in the analysis section was a somewhat scholarly middle aged man who, like himself, felt pressurised by the thrusting young careerists whom he technically outranked but who often bypassed him in seeking management decisions. He was only too pleased to be sidetracked from his routine into what seemed like an amusing diversion.

'Medieval, you say? Now there's a thing. They were keen on codes and ciphers in the Middle Ages. Johannes Tritheminus, Roger Bacon. The famous Roger Bacon. They were great exponents of the cryptic arts.'

'So, it should be easy enough to crack?' said Steiger

'Let me see it. Pictograms rather than letters. Hmmm. That'll make it a bit more difficult, but I'll be delighted to give it a go. The computers should make it a bit easier once I've figured out a sequence or two. Yes. Chaucer, Dante, all your literary greats right down to Shakespeare liked nothing better than a bit of secret writing.'

He gave Steiger a sideways look.

'The... um... what's the word? The provenance of the message would be helpful.'

'In a letter written by a monk to a bishop in fourteenth century Scotland. I don't have the original, I'm afraid,' replied Steiger.

'So, it probably transcribes into Latin rather than English.'

The analyst was speaking to himself rather than Steiger

'But then the cryptograms may just convey ideas or concepts rather than actual words. Yes. Very interesting.'

He addressed Steiger directly.

'I'll give it a go. I'll email you when I've come up with something, or, possibly, nothing.'

He turned to go then paused.

'I assume this is entirely unofficial, off the books, so to speak.'

'Oh sure,' replied Steiger. 'Just a bit of a notion, a whim. Nothing serious. Thanks. I owe you one.'

As the two men parted, the code breaker thought to himself, what was the other up to? With a mental shrug, he dismissed the speculation. It didn't matter to him and it would be nice to have a secret little project all to himself that his brash young colleagues didn't know about.

Pierre Gabrin having concluded his dealings in New York returned to Paris where, in the seclusion of his library, he returned to the parchment. He recalled the parting words of Auguste Daubin. He knew the recipient of the letter but who was the writer, where did he live and why had he, for he was almost certain the writer was male, written it with the coded message to the Bishop of Dunkeld?

Gabrin's knowledge of Scottish history was shaky but he knew that the books and, presumably, the hidden letter were dated to the early fourteenth century. A little superficial research told him of the Wars of Independence with England and the civil wars and internecine struggles in the aftermath. Thus, he reasoned, the letter writer had some information that he wished to impart or something of value that he wished to keep or make safe but why had he chosen the Bishop of Dunkeld as his confidant?

He delved into the internet, giving thought for a moment of how easy it was to find things on the "information highway". What would have taken weeks or months of research in previous years, he could summon to his fingertips in minutes.

The translation of the manuscript had not been easy, but he deduced that the writer was a monk though he had certainly been no Latin scholar. The grammar was flawed. The words "prioratus", "benedictus" and a reference to “insulae sanctorum" seemed to imply that he was writing from a Benedictine priory. The term "insulae sanctorum" translated as "holy island" puzzled Gabrin but with a few key strokes, he was informed that this was the name given to Lindisfarne, an island off the coast of northeast England. He had been told the manuscript was Scottish, so he concluded the source was not the Holy Island but somewhere near, across the border between the countries perhaps.

He trawled through the details of Scottish ecclesiastical establishments near to Lindisfarne and came up with two sites, Tynemouth on the East Lothian Coast and Coldingham close to the ancient port of Berwick upon Tweed. Further study of the manuscript referred to a "hortus conclusus". This, he discovered, was an enclosed garden dedicated to the Virgin Mary.

Both monasteries were Benedictine, both were in Scotland, both were governed by Durham, both dedicated to St. Mary but, in the course of his wanderings through the internet, he had come across a piece of grousing from a medieval monk who seemed to have been sent to Tynemouth as a penance. His grievance was that the house was set on a high rock, was cold, wet and miserable and that he was tired of eating fish. This did not seem like the place for a contemplative garden.

Thus, by a series of exclusions, Pierre Gabrin deduced that the long-deceased correspondent had lived in the Priory of Coldingham. He resolved to visit the place.

CHAPTER 17

The fine mist, a haar in the local idiom, had drifted in from the sea. It happened even on the warmest of days. Two or three miles inland people could be basking in sunshine while this grey wetness hung in the still air clinging to the coast and reducing visibility to a few yards. It made any attempt at bird counts impossible, but Kate reasoned that she could see the stones in a dyke. To get away from it, David had rescheduled his tour to include some inland sites with accompanying tales of jealousy, murder, necromancy and kidnap to spice up the historical facts and would be gone most of the day.

She found the note of the co-ordinates of the last stop on their systematic search of the meandering dykes and field margins of the farms that they had identified as possible locations for the last sighting of the Arrow Stone. They had recently realised that the reference to Northfield encompassed surrounding farms that were now regarded as separate but had previously been regarded as part of the Northfield barony. When multiple permissions had to be sought the farmers had been tolerant, even slightly amused, at their self-made task, extracting promises to share any treasure that might be found and exchanging jokes with their neighbours about the pair.

'I wouldnae mind searchin' ahint a few dykes wi' that lass!'

Suitably clad for the wet weather she set out for the path leading to the heights of Earnsheugh where, judging by the name, sea eagles must have nested in the past. She knew there was a reintroduction programme across the Firth of Forth. As part of her bird count she had been asked to keep a lookout should any, one day, return to their old haunts. Climbing the steep, previously searched field edge to her new starting point, she stopped to try and get a satnav reading on her mobile. As usual the signal was fluctuating. It was then she thought she saw a figure a short distance behind but no sooner had she turned to check than the swirls of mist covered the path.

Just a trick of the haar, she thought and toiled on, up toward the Iron Age forts that David visited in his Discovery field trips and where they had stopped and picnicked on their last search walk when the sun had been warm enough for them to lie on the grass with the coconut scent of the gorse bushes wafting over them.

He had said, 'They call them whins in Scotland. There's always a flower or two on a whin bush even in the winter. There's an old saying "when the whins' no in floo'er, kissing's oot o' season" which, of course, it never is.'

And he had leaned over and kissed her.

That night, she had cooked a meal for them, opened a bottle of wine and when David had declined a second glass on the premise that he was driving she had filled his glass and said, 'You don't have to drive home tonight.'

She was smiling to herself at the recollection of that night when she reached the edge of the field and turned downhill following the wire fence that had long replaced the drystone wall. A few remnants of that old construction, large moss-covered boulders, still lay along the line of the boundary and needed freeing from the grass for inspection. The combination of the wet tendrils of mist sticking her hair to her forehead and the trickles running off her face into the collar of her jacket was becoming a bit tedious and she was beginning to think that the search inspired by a rush of affection for her newly acquired lover wasn't such a good idea after all. She decided to abandon the search and return to the road. She tried again to get a reading on the satnav, gave up and moved off down the slope. Her foot caught on a stone buried in the grass and she tumbled down the slope. Her head struck a fence post and the grey mist became black, then the blackness engulfed her.

She came to and sat up, trying to unscramble her thoughts. Her head was pounding and her hands were scraped raw. She was soaking wet. She tried to stand but lost her balance and was glad to sit down on the wet turf again. She tried again reaching out to the fence for support.

She stood there deciding whether to attempt to walk to the road. She heard voices. Two figures appeared in the mist.

'There she is. Are ye okay, lass?' came a voice.

'Yes. I think so.'

'Can ye walk? Take your time. Here, take a haud o' my airm.'

She recognised the sound of local voices and allowed herself to be led down the field edge to the road where a coastguard Landrover was parked. The engine was running. As she was helped into the vehicle, she was grateful for the blast of warmth from the heater.

'Thank you. Thank you so much,' she said, shivering violently as the heat struck her.

'I've seen you doon at the herbur. You're the lass wi' the kayak.'

'Yes, that's me.' She felt she needed to explain the circumstances

'I was, I was looking for something. A bit stupid now I come to think of it, going out alone in this mist.'

'Aye, the haar can get real thick at times.'

'But how did you know where I was?'

'Now that is a bit odd. An anonymous call went to our co-ordination centre and that's away up in Aiberdeen but the caller was able to give the exact coordinates of where you were.'

'But I was on my own.'

'Well somebody must have seen you but didnae want tae hing aboot so they jist called the coastguard and gave them the exact spot. We're local volunteers so we got the call-oot and set off and, right enough, you were exactly where they said.'

'You must have a guardian angel,' interjected his companion.

Later, after she had reassured David a dozen times that she was fully recovered apart from a bruise the size of a small egg on her forehead just below her hairline, she did repeat the statement as a question.

'So, who is my guardian angel? I did call the coastguard control centre to thank them and try to fish for information about the caller but they said no details were logged, just the information they passed to the volunteers.'

'Did you get their names?' said David. 'We owe them a drink at least.'

'Indeed we do.' she replied

Kate smiled to herself at his use of the word 'we'. It was comforting.

CHAPTER 18

Several days after their encounter Steiger's contact in the cryptanalyst section called and left a message on his voice mail.

'Hi, Brett, I just finished that little job you asked me to do. It was fun. I'd no idea about context so some of it was guess work but I really enjoyed doing it. You did say it was a personal? A whim, I think was the word.'

He sounded a bit arch.

'So, I won't email it. You can buy me a drink and I'll let you have as much as I could work out.'

Later, over some fine whisky, he enthused over the coded message.

'It was a bit difficult. First of all, I guessed the words would be in Latin if it was a substitute cipher, then I reckoned that the symbols might stand for whole ideas or concepts rather than sounds or perhaps both, like hieroglyphs.'

He was assuring Steiger that he had earned the expensive malt he was drinking.

'Then I remembered you saying it was from a monk to a bishop, so I thought, who was using secret codes in the early Middle Ages? Well, we have someone in the frame. Late 12th century. An abbess, Hildegard of Bringen. Saint Hildegard, as she became. She invented a secret language, a *lingua ignota,* with an alphabet of twenty three letters. Anyone in ecclesiastical circles in the next couple of hundred years might have been aware of that or had their own system.'

Steiger sat patiently as his companion indulged his fixation with the cryptographer's art.

'And?' he interjected, prompting.

His companion recognised that perhaps not everyone was as interested in the finer points of ciphers and code breaking, more in the results. He finished his drink and paused. Steiger took the hint and ordered two more.

'Oh. Cheers. This is what I've come up with.'

He placed a sheet of paper on the table between them.

Steiger read:

(The) secret of the order(?) (The) captor of thoughts is safe

Hid(den) in the cave(?) (below ground / buried?)

(The) stone over the door of the monks (priests?) house shows the place

(The) arrow shows the way

'Sorry not a lot but that's as much as I could get out of it.'

He drank his whisky as if Steiger might ask for it back.

'No, no. This is very interesting. Thanks very much I really appreciate all your effort.'

They stood to leave and shook hands.

'Oh, I almost forgot. There were two symbols, or rather one, the same one, at the beginning and the end of the message. I couldn't fit them into any pattern. Both looked like tiny drawings of a skull.'

CHAPTER 19

Pierre Gabrin asked his secretary to book a flight to Edinburgh and told her that he expected to be away on business, probably for a few days but perhaps for a longer time. All messages could be forwarded to his voicemail or personal email if they seemed urgent but otherwise he didn't wish to be contacted or disturbed. He didn't give any reason but his assistant was used to unexplained absences, usually in connection with obscure incidents in his business dealings. She did make a note of the destination. In all the years she had worked for him, she had never known him to visit Scotland.

Brett Steiger had never visited Scotland either. He sat in his office in an anonymous building in Washington while the routine of intelligence gathering and sifting went on in the rooms around him. He read and re-read the strange message. As he promised, he had emailed the contents to Gabrin. He used a personal email address on a private server. After all, he reasoned, this wasn't government business.

Steiger had a quirky mind. Someone had once likened it to a squirrel hiding nuts, burying them around the forest floor seemingly at random but able to find them when needed.

He could remember odd, often apparently unrelated, snippets of information and bring them to the surface when required. It was a valuable tool in the intelligence community. Recalling idiosyncratic facts about individuals, their liking for certain foods or their taste in reading matter, clothes, music or any of a multitude of personal details, could sometimes help to expose a weakness or suggest a line of enquiry or operation.

Of course, all this information was recorded in vast detail and could be searched for if one had a starting point but his ability to short-circuit the data collecting was useful.

Now he was struggling to recall something he had read a long time ago. The mention of the skull symbols had triggered a link to a titbit of information that had been buried for years.

Decades previously, the intelligence communities on all sides had experimented with the possibility of extrasensory perception, psychokinesis and mind reading as tools of espionage and counter espionage. All the lines of enquiry had led down blind alleys with most of the exponents revealed as charlatans or illusionists. There had been some historical research done into recorded episodes of such phenomena but, again, almost all could be attributed to hypnosis, mass hysteria or suggestion. There had even been an investigation into so-called "portals", objects that provided the means by which individuals could harness their powers.

Scrying was the recognised name for this. Nostradamus with his water mirror, the Brahan Seer with his pierced stone and, somewhere in that mass of details, there was a mention of a skull.

Steiger spent several days trawling through old files. Some were so far back they predated the era of computing and, being mostly considered dead ends, had never been considered worthy of the staff time it would take to transcribe them into digital media. To the somewhat bewildered clerks allowing him access to the storage rooms, he explained that he was simply working on a historical treatise, an academic assessment of events long past. His position carried enough clout that no-one questioned his authorisation and his seniority was such that it was quite feasible that, in the twilight of his career, he might undertake such a project, so he was left alone to browse through boxes of fading, yellowing typescript looking for mentions of skulls.

There it was. A few lines in a section dedicated to the use of scrying devices and trials that had been undertaken with volunteers claiming to have clairvoyant or psychic powers. Trials using many methods including breathing techniques, hallucinogenics, and auto-hypnosis had been tried with a variety of mirrors, glass balls, crystals and other objects. All had been failures when subjected to rigorous analysis. A single paragraph mentioned one supposed seer who claimed he had perfected the method used by the Knights Templar in their rituals using a human skull, an art he had discovered in centuries-old accounts of the Crusades written by Egyptian Coptic scholars. He had not been taken very seriously and had indeed been shown to be a charlatan. The overtone of the report was dismissive, and that this information was only included as proof of the thoroughness of the research, presumably to justify to the writer's superiors that he had earned his salary.

Knights Templar? Hmm. That old weasel mentioned a bishop and a monk. In the fourteenth century. Interesting, he thought.

Where had it come from? Scotland. Knights Templar in fourteenth century Scotland.

What has this to do with a skull and why is Gabrin interested?

The natural curiosity of an intelligence agent who had spent a lifetime sifting facts looking for patterns or anomalies was aroused. He grinned to himself.

I'll teach him to use me as a means to an end and then leave me dangling. I think Monsieur Gabrin needs to be followed up.

As Pierre Gabrin was classified as an "asset", all his details were held on file, so it was relatively easy for Steiger to use the facilities of his employers to access his most recent credit card payments. No-one paid much attention to his interest in any one individual. Thousands of such searches were carried out, trawling for information, much of it fruitless.

He noted the flight to Edinburgh. I think I might take a holiday in Bonnie Scotland, mused Steiger. In his youth he had been an enthusiastic skier and still liked a day on the slopes. I'm getting stale stuck in a rut. Maybe it's time for me to go off-piste.

CHAPTER 20

Pierre Gabrin alighted from the plane at Edinburgh airport and with the minimum of delay made his way to the arrivals exit where a taxi driver stood holding a cardboard placard with GABRUN written in felt tip pen. He didn't bother to correct the man. This was probably as close as one could expect from the monoglot British. His secretary's English, though perfect, would have had a Parisian accent. The cab sped along the western approaches to the city and allowed him to appreciate one of the finest city centres in Europe from the main thoroughfare of Princes Street with the open aspect to the castle perched on its crag at the end of the historic Royal Mile. A few manoeuvres to negotiate the convoluted traffic system and he was deposited at the entrance of the Balmoral hotel with its kilted commissionaire in full regalia.

This will make a pleasant base to work from, he thought. Good food, pleasant surroundings. Even if nothing comes of the coded message in the letter, it will have been an enjoyable trip, a new experience, a break from the usual.

Even as he reasoned with himself, he felt the inner desire to find the secret of the manuscript and possess it was more powerful than he expected. It was as if the closer he got to the source of the message the greater the pull became. As someone who cultivated a cool detachment to most of his dealings, he found this feeling slightly unnerving.

A few days later, Brett Steiger booked into the Caledonian Hotel, just the length of Princes Street away from his old acquaintance. From different aspects, both looked out on the brooding fastness of the Castle squatting on its volcanic height but neither could see below the view to the old town in the shadow of the keep, where all the bloody history of Scotland had been played out and where, in earlier times there had been a "house" of the Templars, now obscured and overlaid in the passage of time, buried beneath the growth of the city.

Steiger had let his staff know that, though ostensibly he was on holiday, he wished to be kept informed of the movements of an asset, one Pierre Gabrin. No explanation had been given and none expected but daily, he received a report of credit card activity and so was aware of Gabrin's hiring of a car.

So, he's on the move, is he? But where?

Wishing to keep the whole thing low key and apparently of little significance, he didn't ask for detailed surveillance. He was, after all, on holiday and was, as far as his department was concerned, just making sure he knew the whereabouts of a contact. Nothing more.

The credit card details let him know that Gabrin had lunched some fifty odd miles away before returning, so he thought. Hmm, no harm in taking a little run down the coast myself.

CHAPTER 21

Kate had reassured David for the umpteenth time that she was fully recovered from her fall. Indeed, now that the weather had improved, she had been out in the kayak checking the cliff nest sites. She stated in no uncertain terms that they were going to finish this search and either find the damned Arrow Stone or make certain that it was gone for ever.

David was a little in awe of her. They arranged to recommence from the last point on the satnav. As he climbed to the cliff top, he said,

'Look, this is becoming a bit of an obsession with both of us. I thought it would be a doddle to find it and maybe take a couple of pictures or a quick drawing but it's taking over. Why don't we just give it a rest? For all we know the stone isn't even here anymore.'

'Let's just keep looking.'

Kate didn't know why but this quest had become the most important thing in her life at that moment. She felt she needed to find the stone, not as part of a project or as a bit in a jigsaw or collector's item but as an urge, something atavistic, something in her very being.

They reached the spot where she had tumbled down the slope and she kicked the stone hidden in the long grass that had caught her foot in the mist.

'My god, that's it!' exclaimed David, dropping to his knees to examine the rough-hewn boulder. Pulling it clear of the tussocks and rubbing off the moss with his hand, he revealed the carved outlines on the surface.

'We've found it! You've found it, I should say.'

He grabbed Kate and kissed her.

'You sure?' she said but she knew. It was the stone.

'We found it! We found it!' cried David, raising his arms in triumph.

Kate sat on the hillside looking at the stone and felt it was more that the stone had found her.

CHAPTER 22

Pierre Gabrin found driving on the left disconcerting. How like the British to be out of step with the rest of the world, he thought, as he travelled down the A1. Normally, he liked to think and plan while driving but he was a little afraid to let his thoughts wander while coping with a mirror image of his usual driving technique. As he got used to it, he allowed himself some room for speculation. He was somewhat surprised at his actions. He who normally planned and thought through the consequences and possibilities of even the quickest of decisions had embarked on what he was now beginning to consider a wild goose chase. He had found the enticement of the coded message too much to resist but, in reality, he didn't know what the message was about. What was "the secret of the order"? What on earth did "the captor of thoughts" mean? What he *did* know was that there was a stone involved. A big stone? A stone that is or was over a doorway in some ecclesiastical building and an "arrow pointed the way" but to what and from where was a mystery.

In his long and varied business career Gabrin had bought and sold many commodities including information. He was adept at extracting snippets from various sources and putting together a jigsaw of little pieces to make a picture. A stone and an arrow. Well, that was enough to start with.

He found a comfortable country house hotel with a surprisingly good menu, booked a room then went to the local library. The internet was a valuable resource but not all details were on the net. The library would have a local reference section of older books that might prove a useful start to his search.

CHAPTER 23

David had photographed the stone from every angle, made a sketch of it and even tried to make a rubbing with tracing paper and a wax crayon but the stone was too rough and too wet to make anything of it. Still, he was like a child with a new toy and when Kate suggested they take it back to her cottage, he readily agreed, then he paused in reflection.

'It's too big to carry for any distance and, I suppose, we should ask the landowner. Technically, it belongs to the farm.'

The woman who owned the farm was agreeable but curious about the whole episode.

'No-one's ever asked my permission to take a stone before. It's not a valuable archaeological find is it? You won't be getting the telly people here?'

David reassured her it was just a cup marked stone but that it was an unusual one and he would like to study it a bit more.

'I'll bring it back if you want?'

'Don't be daft. Here hang on. That field is pretty steep. I'll get the quad bike and fetch it down for you.'

Back at the cottage, Kate scrubbed the stone free of the accumulated dirt and moss of years of exposure. She sat looking at it, willing it to reveal its secret.

'What does it mean, do you think?'

'I don't know. There are dozens of theories about these marks. The different types, I mean. Nobody really knows. I just love collecting them. Well, photos of them.'

'Yes, I know, but this one seems different. I've not visited as many sites as you. None at all until this summer, but I've seen all your photos.'

'Yes, apologies for that. Dragging you all over Northumberland. I know I can be a bit of a nerd about these things. You're the first person that hasn't been bored to tears by it. You weren't bored were you?'

'No. I really did find the whole thing interesting, but this stone is different. I just know it.

'Why has it got an arrow? Usually the marks are more... what's the word? Abstract.'

She peered at the stone looking obliquely across the surface.

'See? Just above the point of the arrow. That mark, it looks like a star?'

David came to look.

'Hmm, could just be weather damage or a natural feature. It's very small.'

'I'm sure it's a star.' She looked again.

'And the arrow's pointing to it.'

'People are always seeing more in these marks than are really there. Trying to interpret them with our thinking when, in reality, we don't have a clue about the belief system, the world view of the people who carved them. Think what they would make of a page of squiggles in black ink on a white sheet, yet we can draw on centuries of writing to make meanings from them.'

'I still think it's a star and the arrow points to it.'

'We don't even know if it is really an arrow that is symbolised or if it means something else.'

'Come on, it's an arrow.'

'Alright,' said David, indulgently. 'It's an arrow.'

He lent forward and kissed her.

'Let's give it a rest. Enough for one day. We found the Arrow Stone. Let's celebrate.'

'Okay. There's a bottle of Merlot in the kitchen and glasses on the drainer.'

'You know that this means you can't drive home, again.'

'Oh dear,' he replied in mock surprise. 'I hadn't thought of that!'

'You chancer,' she said punching his arm.

CHAPTER 24

Pierre Gabrin's instincts had proved successful. In the small local library, he had sought out the "Local" section and asked the librarian where he might find references to ancient stones.

'There are several works dealing with local aspects of geology. No? There are very detailed lists of gravestones in all the old churchyards. There are one or two books about prehistoric tumuli and standing stones.'

Gabrin grimaced. This wasn't going to be as easy as he thought.

The librarian noticed his expression and said helpfully, 'The best place to start might be the Proceedings of the Antiquarians. There are many volumes but there is a separate index. If you just look under "stone" you might get a starting point.'

She indicated a row of identically bound volumes with a slightly slimmer one at the end marked "Index".

Gabrin thanked her with a slight bow and crossed to the shelf. He took out the index, opened it and ran his finger down the column of entries for "stone(s)" and gave an intake of breath. He couldn't believe his luck. There it was. A single line

Arrow Stone, The. Vol. III Ch. 14.

He pulled volume III from the line of books and flicked over the pages and read the entry with regard to the location of the stone. He scribbled a note of the details and replaced the book.

'Did you find what you were looking for?'

The librarian looked up from her computer screen.

'I think so. Possibly. I wonder, please, is there anyone in the area who is an expert, or has a special interest, in antiquities?' he asked.

She thought, staring into the middle distance.

'Yes,' she pointed to the noticeboard.

'Him. Them. They do tours. There on the board. See?'

Gabrin crossed the room and read,

East Borders Bespoke Archaeological Discovery Tours. (EBBA Discovery Tours) Tour Guide - David Morton.

He made a note of the details with the thought that this chap might be useful. He didn't know how true this would turn out to be.

CHAPTER 25

Kate woke with a start and sat up in bed, her red hair in a tousled beehive.

'It's a map!'

She shook the sleeping David into semi-wakefulness. 'I know what the stone means. It's a map!'

'Wha...what are you speaking about? Wha...what time is it?'

'Three o'clock. Wake up. I've solved it. It sort of came to me in a dream.'

David slowly surfaced from sleep.

'What are you talking about? It's the middle of the night.'

'The stone. The Arrow Stone. It's a map.'

David raised himself on to an elbow, then sat up and rubbed his eyes.

'Oh, I see. This is no big deal. There are dozens of theories about cup and ring markings as maps. Astronomical charts. Sites of copper deposits. All sorts of ideas.'

'No. No. I don't mean that. I mean it's a real map. It's not one of your cup and ring stones. That's what it's meant to look like, but you said yourself, it's like nothing you've ever come across. That's because it's not the same. It's a real map of a place or places. That's why it's got an arrow on it. You said none of the others, anywhere in the world, has an arrow.'

'You mean it's a fake.'

'Well, yes. No, not really. It just meant to look like one of your stones for some reason, I don't know why, but it's a map. Maybe only one person knew about it. I don't know but I'm sure it's a map. Get up. Let's go and look at it again.'

'It's quarter past three.'

'Get up.'

In the sitting room, David raked the embers of the stove and added some dry sticks, beachcombed some days earlier to get a blaze going. A "tuppenny" fire some old man had once called it.

Kate was poring over the digital images of the stone, her auburn tresses hiding her face.

'See. This long wiggly line. That could be a river or a stream. Those spirals could be hills.'

'Well, that's really helpful. A stream or a river beside some hills. That really pinpoints things. Not many of them about.'

'Don't scoff. I'm sure I'm right. Just before I woke up, it was clear as day.'

'And now?'

'It'll come to me. Concentrate. Think.'

She screwed her eyes shut trying to remember the dream. A dream already fading into vague images.

'The arrow doesn't seem to point to anything. You'd think it would if it was a map.'

'It does. See? That little cross thing?'

'X marks the spot!'

'If you're just going to joke about this...'

'No. No. I am taking it seriously. Let me see the pictures.'

David examined the pictures he had downloaded on to Kate's computer. He used the magnifier on them then went over and did the same to the stone itself with an old magnifying glass.

'That mark isn't a cross. It's got five points. It's a star. The arrow is pointing to a star. Why a star?'

After a moment's thought, he exclaimed, 'The Pole star. Polaris. Due north.'

'What do you mean?'

'If it is a map as you say then the arrow is a sort of compass needle. It points north, to the Pole star, so you know which way up to look at it.'

He paused as his newfound enthusiasm abated.

'Doesn't help much though. We know which way up it goes but no clues as to where it is.'

Kate made a sort of counting motion with her fingers.

'We can assume it's somewhere local. There would be no point in making a map of somewhere far away. It's old. So, what is the oldest building in the area? The Priory. Most likely came from the Priory. Agreed?'

'Possibly. Probably. Maybe just possibly.'

'What did the book say about it?'

David rubbed his forehead, remembering.

'It was a door lintel in the old mansion house at Templehall which was burned down then it got used to make a dyke.'

'And where did a lot of the stone used to build old houses come from?'

'The Priory ruins before conservation was thought about.'

'Exactly.' concluded Kate.

'It's a bit tenuous but, I admit, it's possible. Okay, you've got a Priory connection. It is four thirty. Let's sleep on it. Let's go back to bed.'

'To sleep on it?'

David grinned.

CHAPTER 26

David was pleased with life. He had a beautiful redheaded girlfriend who was genuinely interested in his, by his own admission nerdy, obsession with petroglyphs and he had found the Arrow Stone. Strictly speaking, it had been Kate who had found it but that made its discovery even more special. He could hardly keep from grinning to himself. Life was so good.

One can't live on happiness alone. He still had to earn his living, meagre though it was, but he was still smiling inwardly as he went to meet his new group of history buffs looking for an armchair discovery tour. The tours were customised to meet the needs and abilities of each group and the vagaries of the weather. The day was as sunny as his mood and the customers were a fairly fit looking bunch, so he planned to take them over the border to see standing stones and battlefields that required a bit of legwork. Standing at his preferred starting point at Coldingham Priory, he was giving his introductory talk about what they might expect to see when a dapper little gentleman with a hint of an accent asked him if they would be seeing any cup and ring marked stones.

David said that the best ones were a little bit too far to include in the pre-arranged tour but if there was enough interest, he could organise a trip specifically on that topic.

'I'll pass round a sheet later and if you would like me to, I'll do a one-off special.'

Nothing was too much trouble for him in his benign mood and an extra trip meant extra fees.

'I have a special interest in such stones.'

'Oh, me too,' replied David pleased to find a fellow enthusiast.

'Yes. In fact, I have just been reading about one in this area, one called the Arrow Stone? Have you come across such a stone?'

David felt his stomach flip over. He was about to blurt out Kate's theory and invite the stranger to see their prize when a twinge of doubt stopped him. It seemed an outrageous coincidence that he should be asked about the stone the day after they had spent hours deciding if the stone was a map or held a message of some sort.

Having confessed a special interest, he couldn't deny all knowledge. Trying to keep his face noncommittal, he replied.

'Of course. Yes, I've heard of it. It is, or rather it seems from the description to be an unusual example,' he said trying to create the impression that he had never actually seen such a stone.

Gabrin caught the momentary change in his expression. He said nothing but wondered to himself what this young man was keeping to himself about the Arrow Stone.

'And skulls, or maybe just one skull. Do any of these stones have skulls on them?'

David knew then that he had been fishing with his declared interest in cup marked stones. Anyone with any knowledge of them would know the answer,

'No. None I've ever heard of.'

'Any stones with skulls carved on them in this area?'

David inclined his head over his shoulder.

'Take your pick in the graveyard or any of the kirkyards around here. Our forefathers weren't as squeamish about death as we are. There are quite a few gravestones with skulls on them, and bones too.'

'From the fourteenth century?'

What an odd question, thought David.

'No. Oh my goodness, no. The earliest are eighteenth century.'

Then he thought, why not push the visitor for his real reasons behind the questions.

'What's your interest in carvings of skulls?' he said, adding the sweetener, 'If I can help in any way?'

Gabrin looked at him. He was used to making decisions about contacts, their honesty and motives. He decided that he had to gamble a bit. Let this young man have some information then find out what he knew.

'I have seen a document. A letter which is thought to have been written here in the fourteenth century. It refers to skulls or a skull. It is difficult to say exactly. It was of course written a long time ago and in Latin, so the translation may be imperfect.'

He chose to omit that the reference was in code.

'There was a mention of an order, presumably a holy order and...'

He took a calculated risk to gauge David's reaction.

'...a secret of some kind, apparently connected with a skull in some way. The document was of a fragmentary nature.'

By this time David was master of his expression but his pulse was racing.

'Intriguing. I can see why you're interested in this part of the Priory and this part of the world but what connection is there with...'

He feigned difficulty in remembering.

'…this Arrow Stone. You mentioned that earlier. I don't see the connection.'

'Perhaps there isn't one,' said Gabrin watching for any flicker in David's expression like a poker player trying to read his opponent. 'I just came across a mention of it in some research I had been doing.'

'Well, I'll give it some thought and the idea of a skull carving or whatever and I'll let you know if there is anything I can think of. You're staying locally? Mr... or is it Monsieur?'

'Gabrin,' replied his interlocutor, 'Pierre Gabrin.'

It was the longest day of David's life. He had to take his group through all the sites and sights of the trip with his explanations and answers to every query, all the time keeping an eye on Gabrin and yet trying to act as though the questions posed had no special significance.

He couldn't wait to get back to Kate and give her all the details.

'What? He actually asked about the Arrow Stone? That's got to be more than a coincidence. We've not mentioned the name of it to anyone, not even whatsername, the nice lady with the quad bike, the farm lady. We didn't call it the Arrow Stone when we asked to shift it, did we?'

'No, I'm sure we didn't. It *could* just be a coincidence.'

'No. This is most odd. What's he like, and what was all that about skulls?'

'I don't know. He's ordinary looking. Foreign accent. French, I think. And there's no carved skull anywhere on the Arrow Stone or on any petroglyph I know of though there are plenty on old graves.'

Kate looked pensive.

'But he said something about the skulls being mentioned in a fourteenth century document.

'When you see him for the next trip, ask him directly about the document and ask him if it mentions the stone. There's nothing like the direct approach. No need to tell him we have it. That can wait until we see what he has to say.'

She laughed.

'This is getting quite exciting.'

Exciting was not the word David would have used.

CHAPTER 27

Brett Steiger was quite enjoying himself. He had mounted a one man surveillance operation on Pierre Gabrin. It took him back to his young self when he had first started in counter-intelligence. His active phase hadn't lasted long. He had talent for administration, for files and paper trails that now had digital footprints. He had been desk bound for years but it was nice to try and recall the training and to play a little game with the unsuspecting Gabrin.

At first, he had thought that perhaps his quarry was taking a genuine if unusual, holiday. He knew Gabrin did have a real interest in history and was a collector of ancient documents so maybe this was just another collecting trip. Then he read the brochure and its mention of Coldingham Priory as a "fourteenth century monastic establishment".

He recalled Gabrin's voice,

"The letter was written by a monk in fourteenth century Scotland".

So that's why he's here, he thought. Somehow Gabrin had deduced that the letter originated in the Priory and he was trying to follow up a seven hundred year old trail.

The best of luck, buddy, he chuckled to himself.

He resurrected his old skills enough to watch Gabrin in conversation with the young man acting as tour guide. He also noted that the Levantine businessman's questions took far longer than the others in the group.

What's he quizzing the guy about?

In fact, the reverse was the case. David was engaging Gabrin in conversation as suggested by Kate.

'The other day, you were asking about the stone called the Arrow Stone. You mentioned a document. A letter. Is there a mention of such a stone in the letter?'

'No, no.' replied Gabrin, caught slightly off guard.

He paused, then decided that apparent openhandedness might be worthwhile. After all, the young man had brought the subject up so he must have an interest in, or knowledge of, the stone though he had been cagey about it before. Gabrin had noticed the flicker on his features when he first heard the name. He would feed some information, just enough to give the impression of co-operation and see what was offered in return.

'The letter mentions "a stone from the door of the monks' place" and "an arrow showing the way". That's why I latched on to the idea of this Arrow Stone. The letter mentions a secret, hidden. Underground. Buried or in a tomb...'

He thought for a moment.

'...or in a cave. Are there any caves in this area?'

'Not really. Wrong sort of geology. There are a few but they're really overhanging rock shelves rather than deep caves. There are sea caves along the cliffs but they're mostly tidal. Full of sea water at high tide. No. I can't think of any. No tombs neither.'

'Oh well. If anything comes to mind or if you know of anyone who might help, let me know.'

Gabrin watched David's face trying to read him and was sure there was something he wasn't disclosing but concluded that he, Pierre Gabrin, could play cat and mouse games better than anyone especially better than this young tour guide. He could wait.

Back at the cottage, David recounted the results of his conversation with Gabrin.

'You were right. The direct approach worked. Well, sort of. He said the document mentioned "a stone from the door of monks' place" and "an arrow shows the way" but no direct mention of the Arrow Stone. He also mentioned a secret that was buried or in a tomb or a cave. He asked if there were any caves around here. Well, there aren't. I told him. Wrong sort of geology. Just a few sea caves.'

'And no mention of skulls?' said Kate.

'He didn't say anything and, to be frank, I was so anxious about what I should or shouldn't say and trying to make mental notes of what he was saying that I didn't ask him,' confessed David.

Kate thought it over.

'So, the Arrow Stone isn't specifically referred to in his document but “a stone from the door" could be a lintel and we know the stone was a lintel at least once. An arrow showing the way. There must be a connection. It's too much of a coincidence not to be. The stone must be some kind of map but what for and where?'

David stared into the driftwood fire recalling his conversation, searching for clues in the answers.

'What was that about a secret? A secret what? Buried or underground in a tomb or cave. Where could that be? A tomb? A cave?'

Kate looked up, eyes wide.

'That's it. You said it. Sea caves. There are plenty of them along the cliffs.'

She stopped then carried on, her voice becoming more animated.

'The map. The lines on the Arrow Stone. The wiggly line across it. It isn't a river. It's the coastline. The coastline looking north. The arrow shows the way. That's what the document said.'

David thought it over.

'Yes, that could be it. We haven't any idea of scale and there is a lot of coast. What could you put in sea cave? It would be washed out at the first tide.'

'Stop making objections. Get back to your place and fetch your maps of the area. I'm going to make a tracing of that wiggly line and see if it fits any part of the coast. Go on. This is getting so exciting.'

David noted that was the second time she had used that expression.

CHAPTER 28

Back in his hotel Gabrin lingered over his evening meal. The food was good, and the wine list well chosen. He was beginning to revise his preconceived notions of Scottish cuisine.

He was also reviewing his ideas about David Morton and what he knew about the secret of the letter with the skulls. He resolved to watch him and note where he went.

If he thinks I'm on to him and if he knows where the secret is hidden, he'll go and check it. It's human nature. Misers are always checking their hidden gold in case anyone has found it. I'll keep an eye on him.

There was something about this whole venture. He couldn't explain it, even to himself. Since his arrival in the area, he had been aware of a vague feeling of unrest. Usually he was calculating and dispassionate about his affairs. Business, his collections, even his sexual liaisons all gave him a sense of fulfilment and pleasure, but it was always at one remove. His inner being, his core, remained detached.

This was different. There was something at the back of his mind that he couldn't quite conceptualise, something atavistic, a wraith of feeling with no words.

The fragments of an ancient strain were creating echoes behind his conscious thoughts. He knew he had to find the secret. He would watch the man he felt sure would lead him to that secret. A secret that he had to uncover. Why it assumed such importance he didn't know and didn't understand but the desire burned within him.

Brett Steiger sat in his hotel with a large malt whisky, mulling over the events he'd witnessed. The conversation between Gabrin and the tour guide. He missed having the advantage of the arsenal of surveillance techniques available to State counter-intelligence. The exchange could have been overheard, recorded and replayed like so many others he had been privy to, but this operation was, he reminded himself, strictly off piste.

Still, there were advantages on this trip. The hotel stocked one of the finest collections of malt whiskies he had ever seen and a very knowledgeable barman. Steiger was getting a geography lesson as he travelled from the peaty malts of Islay, by way of Skye and Orkney, through the Highlands to Speyside and down to the Lowlands. He would give it another week, he reckoned. That was about as long as he could play the game of being on holiday. He didn't really have much to go on. A hunch. A gut feeling that Gabrin was on to something. Another week then he'd have to give up or pass it on through the official channels which he didn't fancy. Trying to explain to hard-headed sceptical colleagues why they should bother with a fourteenth century letter would expose him to not a little ridicule.

Another week. Nothing for it. He'd just have to keep up observation on Gabrin and see what transpired.

The watcher was to be watched.

CHAPTER 29

David arrived at Kate's cottage. He was spending as much time there as at his own but somehow they still kept their lives a bit separate. Neither of them had said anything but it seemed the right arrangement for the time being.

As the originator of the theory of a map on the stone, Kate took charge of the investigation.

'Spread the map out on the table. We'll start locally. It would seem logical for the map to be somewhere nearby unless the stone was meant to be read by someone going on a journey but since they couldn't take the stone with them, it follows that it was meant to be read here.

Right. You think…we think, the arrow points to the north. I've changed my mind about the river idea and think the wiggly line represents the coastline. Okay?'

'So far, so good,' said David, 'But there is the question of scale. A detailed map of a short stretch of coastline with every little outcrop might be different or the same as a less specific map of a longer stretch.'

'Stop raising objections before we've even started. Here, I've traced the outline from the Arrow Stone, let's look at the map and see if it fits any of it. If the arrow does show the way, then it's only the northern coast we need to look at.'

They pored over the O.S. map of the area with the traced outline from the stone carving alongside, one dark and one red head almost touching.

David traced the coastline with his index finger.

'The scale isn't right' he said in exasperation. 'If this is a coastline, it is on a much bigger scale than the map.'

'Keep looking,' said Kate. 'You know this area so well. You've driven along the cliff tops with your tour parties. Look for an anomaly. Sometimes, when I was doing bird counts, I would look for an unusual rock feature on a cliff to act as a marker and work from that.'

After a long period of silence punctuated by little 'tuts' of concentration, David said,

'I think…it might be. I'm not sure, but…yes…maybe.'

'Oh, get on. Where?'

David pointed with the end of a pencil.

'I think that could be Fast Castle Head. See, if that spiral is a hill then this could be the Head with those two small circles for outliers, offshore rocks. The line going at an angle to the main one could be the path to the Head. The road from the moor. This other deep short cut line could be the dean that runs down to the cliffs. Yes, the more I look at it, the more I think it could be Fast Castle Head. That cup mark could represent the castle itself.'

Kate looked at the map and then back to the tracing.

'You've got it!' she said and hugged him.

She peered at the tracing then went over to the stone itself and peered as closely at it with the magnifying glass.

'Get those photographs you took up on the computer and get some magnification on them. There's a mark, close to the line. I'm sure there is. It looks like a cross.'

'X marks the spot, you said that before but that was a star.'

'This isn't an X either. It's not a times sign. It's a plus sign. Well, it is a little cross with...' She looked closely at the stone then at the enlarged digital image. '…the ends of the arms are sort of splayed out. It looks deliberate because the cross is tiny compared to the rest of the carving but is obvious.'

David scrutinised the enlarged image.

'Could be just the effect of weathering. Even if this is not a genuine Neolithic carving, it is still pretty old and it's been lying about in walls and fields for centuries. Still, a cross pattee, as it's called, is quite medieval. Crusaders and all that. It's also the shape of the German medal, the Iron Cross'

'Enough of the lectures. What do you think it could mean?'

Kate looked at him, her eyes bright.

'This is getting exciting again.'

David felt a flicker of disquiet. That was the third time she had used the word. He was not sure where this adventure was leading and if he was ready for it.

He concentrated on the map.

'The cross thing is just alongside the wiggly line that we have decided is a coastline. It is almost touching it so whatever it represents must be at the foot of the cliffs, if our suppositions about the wiggly line are correct.'

'What would you find at the foot of a cliff? A wreck, perhaps?'

David looked again at the enlarged image.

'There's an indentation, a small, deep cup mark right on the line. In fact, the line runs through it.'

He snapped his fingers.

'Of course, the French guy, when he was asking about skulls, said something was buried or in a tomb, or in a cave!'

'That must be it. There must be a cave at the foot of the cliff.'

David grimaced.

'Oh there will almost certainly be a cave somewhere along there. More than one, most likely, but they're sea caves. They will be under water at high tide and the sea rushes in and out. There couldn't be anything in there or, if there was, it was washed out into the North Sea centuries ago.'

'We could go and look,' said Kate in a wheedling tone. 'No harm in having a look.'

'Well, I'm not so sure about "no harm",' said David. 'Those cliffs are dangerous. Very high and very steep. Even if you get down, it's easy to get trapped by the tide and difficult, if not impossible, to climb back. It is not easy or safe to approach by boat. There are surges and hidden rocks. Even the crab boats give it a wide berth. And these guys know the sea.'

'I've kayaked around the coast all summer.' replied Kate with the hint of a pout. 'I could go on my own if you're not keen.'

David knew that by 'not keen' she meant scared and he felt challenged by this girl who had totally captivated him but about whom, he was realising, he knew very little.

'Okay. We'll take a look-see along the coast below the cliffs but full warning, I'm in charge, I know the lie of the land and what I say goes. No foolhardiness. These cliffs really are dangerous. We wait until we get a calm day. No point in getting blown over by a gale and we give ourselves plenty of time to avoid tides. They can rise fairly quickly and cut you off.'

'Message received and understood. Dib dib dib, dob dob dob, or whatever it is they say.You are the leader.' She grinned and added, 'It suits you being all masterful.'

Once more, he was left wondering. This girl was as puzzling as she was attractive. A delightful puzzle but then, he'd always enjoyed puzzles.

CHAPTER 30

Brett Steiger swirled his whisky round in the glass. He gently inhaled the bouquet and then added a drop of water. The barman with his vast experience of uisge beatha, the water of life, had assured him that this was quite permissible to release the subtlety of the flavours.

'Room temperature mind.' he had said. 'Not chilled and certainly never with ice.'

The American smiled at the pride the Scot had shown in his national drink and how he had quoted the Scottish author James Hogg, saying that if a man could discover the right proportion and quantity to drink daily and keep to that, he might live forever.

'The problem's aye been finding the right proportion,' he had concluded with a grin, 'and keepin' to it.'

Steiger had had an enjoyable trip but, as he acknowledged to himself, not a very successful one so far. He turned the facts over in his mind. He had some idea about the meaning of the skull symbols in the code but not much more than Gabrin had told him. Gabrin had somehow worked out that the original letter had originated in the Priory at Coldingham.

The young man that Gabrin had been in conversation with had obviously something to do with the secret, whatever it was, but Steiger, lacking his surveillance equipment, had been unable to find out.

He sipped his dram and reviewed his options. He could return home. Before leaving, he could take in one of the whirlwind tours of the sights so popular with visitors. He could approach the young man directly and declare his interest in whatever Gabrin had asked about. Neither of these appealed to him as a course of action.

He decided that his best bet was to engineer a meeting with Gabrin, expressing surprise at the coincidence of their both being there. He could then ask if Gabrin was following up the manuscript lead and offer to help using his information about the skull symbol as a bargaining chip. He knew Gabrin would know that it was no coincidence and that Steiger had an interest in finding out the secret but would play along with the offer of help. They had worked together in the past to their mutual benefit and the Levantine would accept his input. Steiger felt he knew his man and what motivated him.

What he didn't know, what he couldn't know, what even Gabrin was unaware of, was the stirring that was the latent ability coded in the Levantine businessman's genome. The imprint of the Watcher's race, hidden for millennia, could still be felt.

The American planned the "coincidence" of his meeting Gabrin with great care. He rehearsed his background story in his mind, checked the hotel where he knew the other man was staying and managed to find out that he intended to lunch at the hotel the next day.

Later, he phoned the reception desk and booked a meal for two. He knew Gabrin would check on him. His cover was that he had arranged to meet a family history researcher who, for a fee, would do all the ground work in tracing someone's ancestry.

He had arrived to discuss the details, but the ancestor-tracker had called off at the last minute leaving him to lunch alone. At this point, he would see his old acquaintance Pierre Gabrin and invite him to share his table.

He knew perfectly well that Gabrin wouldn't believe a word of the story but felt he would be intrigued enough to go along with it to find out how much Steiger knew. He would know that Steiger would know that as well. They had both spent a long time in the world of known unknowns and unknown unknowns where truths and half-truths, lies and suspicions of lies were filtered through the sieve of pragmatism.

Steiger arranged to be at his table before the other was due and was browsing through some pages of purported family history that he had cobbled up from the internet.

He looked up as Gabrin entered the dining room.

'Well, blow me! Pierre!'

Gabrin stopped at the familiar voice and turned to stare at Steiger.

'Pierre Gabrin. I can't believe it. What on earth brings you here?'

Momentarily taken aback, Gabrin stared at him then recovered his wits quickly enough to sidestep the question and turn it back.

'Steiger. Brett Steiger. I might well ask you the same question.'

'Me? Oh, chasing up some family history. My great grandmother came from hereabouts it seems.'

Every other American he knew seemed to have a Scottish grandmother, so this seemed a reasonable piece of family background.

'On my mother's side, of course.'

He realised that even Gabrin would be aware that there weren't many Steigers in the Scottish Borders.

Gabrin smiled and nodded, not believing a word of it.

'How interesting, and what a coincidence us both being in the same hotel.'

'Yes. Yes, indeed. I'm not staying here. I was supposed to meet this family history guy for lunch, but he's not shown for whatever reason. I've given up on him. I was about to eat. The table's booked for two. Why don't you join me?'

Gabrin paused, gave an almost imperceptible shrug then pulled out a chair and sat down opposite.

'Thank you. I was going to lunch here anyway.'

Steiger knew that his old acquaintance didn't believe his story but, as he had calculated, was prepared to go along with it. Gabrin sat down, thinking how to play this particular game. Steiger must have come because of the coded message. He knew very little of the original document so he must have something extra or something new about the solution to the code. Gabrin decided that in order to find out what that was, he would have to exchange a certain amount of information in return.

'So, have you progressed far with your search?'

'Search?'

'For your forefathers or foremothers. You said something about a grandmother.'

'Oh, that. No, not much luck. This chap I was to meet, the family history search guy...'

His sentence trailed off as they both kept up the charade of why Steiger was there while each looked for an opening for the exchange of information they both sought.

'...and you? You still haven't said what brings you here. Researching any interests of your own?' said Steiger, giving the other man an opportunity to raise the subject they were verbally circling.

Gabrin paused, thought then decided that his calculated course of action was the correct one.

'Yes. As a matter of fact I am. Do you remember the document I asked your help with? The one with the cipher in it?'

'Yes, I remember it,' said Steiger as though it were a vague memory.

'Well, I did some research and concluded it originated here or, at least, near here. At Coldingham Priory to be exact.'

'I'm impressed,' replied Steiger, wondering how much he needed to hear before offering his ideas about the skull symbol.

'I remember now. You did say the letter was from a monk to a bishop. Was the bishop in charge of this priory place?'

'No, priories have priors at their head. The letter was written *to* a bishop in Dunkeld but the important bit is where it was *from* and that seems to be here. The monk was telling the bishop something about a secret that was here or at least near here.'

'But you don't know what the secret is,' said Steiger who now saw his chance to play his trump card. 'Do you remember there were skull symbols at the beginning and end of the cipher?'

'Ye-es,' replied Gabrin, pulling thoughtfully at his lower lip.

'Well, I gave them some thought after you'd gone. Couldn't get them outta my mind. Something was nagging in my brain. It took ages but finally, I found a connection. Well, I think it's a connection.'

Gabrin leaned forward in his chair. All the ambiguity of their early conversation was forgotten. Steiger expounded his ideas about the use of a skull as a scrying portal, as a facilitator to mind reading.

'The "captor of thoughts". Isn't that what the cipher said?'

'A skull?' said Gabrin. 'Skulls are commonplace. At one time every medical student had one. Two if you count his own! Museums are chock full of them to say nothing of monasteries and catacombs. It can't mean just a skull.'

'According to this guy, there was a special skull. The Knights Templar made use of it.'

'Not the Templars! They are always cited as the origin of every crackpot theory and idea.'

'I know. I know. I was as sceptical as you are but then I thought what the hell, maybe there is something in it.'

Remembering his alleged reason for being there, he added.

'I was going to contact you with the details after I got back from this trip.'

Gabrin smiled across the table. He didn't believe a word of the American's story of researching family history and realised that he had been traced and followed. Steiger must have gone to a lot of trouble to find him so he must find the idea of this special skull conferring the ability to read thoughts credible.

Gabrin was deeply suspicious of the whole idea but, try as he might, he couldn't see any advantage to the other man in lying to him nor could he see any disadvantage to himself with going along with it.

Steiger had obviously decided he needed Gabrin's help and, if he was honest, he wasn't progressing very fast himself so a little assistance might not come amiss. He smiled again, more broadly, and said,

'You are suggesting that we join forces to find the secret of the parchment?'

Steiger nodded.

'Yes. Like old times. We pool our information and take it from there whether this skull idea turns out to be a nonsense or not.'

He wished to give the impression that he had more to add to the enterprise than his theory about the skull. Gabrin was still suspicious of the other's motives and loyalties but decided to go along with the plan if only to see where it might lead.

'You seriously expect me to believe that the Knights Templar are at the back of this?'

'I know. It sounds like a kid's video game. Hunt the Skull. But let's take it from there for the moment,' replied Steiger.

'Okay, but I was expecting something a bit more realistic. Something with a more...'

He sucked his teeth.

'...monetary value.'

'You're a collector,' said Steiger. 'Maybe there's some great historical artefact just waiting for you to find it.'

'From the little I've read about the time when the letter was written, fourteenth century Scotland, there seems to have been nothing except battles and carnage for the entire century, so I don't think there were many precious artworks created then but who knows, perhaps we will find out.'

He stretched out his hand to shake that of the American.

'We have a deal.'

The two then proceeded to order lunch and continued to exchange titbits of information. Gabrin quickly realised that Steiger had brought very little to the game and spent the entire meal calculating how much he needed to tell him to get his support. The fact that Steiger had sought him out gave him the upper hand but he would need the other to act as a sounding board for his ideas and for his expertise in collating facts into a coherent whole. He was also aware that David Morton may have had his suspicions aroused by his questioning about the Arrow Stone but had not met Steiger so might be less guarded if approached by him.

He explained his theory about the Arrow Stone being somehow part of the riddle and that the young tour guide seemed to know about it though he hadn't said as much.

'I can capture some thoughts without the aid of any skull other than my own,' he said, tapping his temple.

'His face gave him away when I mentioned it. He tried to hide it but I saw the change. He knows something about the stone and maybe he has worked out what the meaning of it is.'

Steiger thought, then spoke.

'But you've not seen it?'

Gabrin grimaced and shook his head.

'So, the first thing is to find out if the kid has the stone or knows where it is and then we've got to get a look at it and make our own deductions. Yeh?'

He looked from beneath his furrowed brow at the other man.

'How do we do that?' inquired Gabrin.

'Oh, a little burglary might be called for. Let's find out where he lives for a start.'

Gabrin dabbed his mouth fastidiously with his napkin.

'Sounds more in your line than mine.'

'That's why we make a good team,' said Steiger, relieved to have cemented the partnership.

CHAPTER 31

David and Kate made plans for an exploration of the cliffs around Fast Castle.

'We'll need torches. Several.' said David.

'You certainly have a grasp of the obvious.' replied Kate.

He ignored the jibe.

'Head torches to leave hands free.' he added.

'Wetsuits or better still, drysuits. Have you got one?' said Kate. 'I've a spare for the kayak but I doubt it'll fit you!'

'No, never needed one. Do I really need one for this?'

'Nothing better for crawling about in sea water. We can hire one at the surf shop by the beach, and bootees. Maybe trainers would do.'

She pondered for a moment then said 'Helmets? No, I think we can do without them.'

'Don't get carried away,' said David. 'We're only going to peer into a few caves. Probably without success.'

'Don't be such a killjoy. Look upon it as an adventure.'

'An adventure? Is that what it is? You make it sound like something out of Enid Blyton.'

'I liked Enid Blyton. The Mountain of Adventure, the Castle of Adventure, the River of Adventure. I read them all.'

'Alright, point taken. This is an adventure, but we better take a rope, just in case of misadventure. I've got one from the days when I did some rock climbing on the cliffs. Remind me to pick it up from the cottage after we get all the rest of the gear.'

They climbed into Kate's little car and drove to Berwick to purchase head torches from the outdoor activities store and then detoured to the surfing centre to hire a suit for David.

By the time their various chores were completed, it was evening and Kate suggested fish and chips back at her cottage.

'The rope!' exclaimed David.

Kate turned the car on to the moors road towards his cottage. A cottage that was fast becoming merely a storage facility for David's possessions, so much time was he spending at her place.

David turned the key in the lock. As he went through the main room of the little house, he sensed something was wrong. Things were not just as they should have been. Nothing specific, just a feeling that some of the few items around the room had been moved. Notes for his coach trip talks stacked by the chair by the fireplace seemed different and one or two reference books left open on a table were not quite as he remembered them.

'Kate,' he called. 'I think someone's been in here.'

'What? What makes you think that?'

'It's nothing I can put my finger on. It just seems different.'

'Anything missing?'

'No. I don't think so. In fact, everything looks alright but just a bit different.'

'You're sure? Why would anyone break in and not take anything?'

She glanced around.

'Not that there's much to take.'

'That's it. That's what's so odd. There isn't much but if it was a burglary, it was expertly done. There's no sign of any "breaking and entering" and why not take the binoculars that I keep for the field trips. Four pairs. They would be worth something.'

Kate shrugged.

'Maybe you're just imagining it,' she said.

'It's been a while since you've been back here,' she added playfully.

'Maybe. Maybe that's it,' said David but, as he left, he frowned and looked round the room again. He was sure he wasn't imagining things.

They left for Kate's via the chip shop, but David couldn't dismiss the niggling feeling that something wasn't quite as it should be and he began to make connections with the Arrow Stone. Could the discovery of the stone be connected in some way and what about Monsieur Gabrin and his odd questions? Could he be involved? Had there really been someone in his cottage or did he just imagine it and, if there had been, what were they doing there?

CHAPTER 32

Brett Steiger and Pierre Gabrin faced each other across the small table in the lounge of Steiger's hotel. Steiger continued his exploration of the Scottish malt whiskies while Gabrin nursed a brandy. They sat in studied silence for a while then Gabrin spoke.

'I admire your skill as a picker of locks. You're quite the Raffles. Have you thought of a second career?'

'That cottage lock could have been opened with a toothpick!' snorted Steiger. 'It was hardly worth his while closing the door.'

'And hardly worth our while getting in,' concluded Gabrin.

'At least we know it's not there.'

'We don't even know if he has it or, indeed, if the so-called Arrow Stone has anything to do with the letter or the secret and we don't know what that is or was, even if it still exists.'

'So many unknowns,' laughed Steiger. 'Just the sorta territory we are used to. Eh?'

'Indeed,' said his companion, his tone lightening. 'As you said. Like old times'

The American sipped his Cardhu thoughtfully.

'He has a girl. At least I've seen him with one. A redhead.'

Gabrin looked up with interest.

'Yeah,' continued Steiger. 'While I was...'

He didn't like to admit to his surveillance of Gabrin. Not to his face.

'...searching out my ancestry. I saw them together. Of course, I didn't know who he was then.'

Gabrin chose to ignore the gaping holes in the continuing fabrication of Steiger's family history search. He knew Steiger must have seen the girl when he was keeping watch on himself and David Morton, but he chose to ignore this and go along with the other's account.

'This redhead? Are you suggesting she might be involved with the stone in some way?'

'Maybe she's got it. Whatever, we need to find out more about her.'

'Indeed,' said Gabrin, then went on.

'I understand there are more redheads in Scotland and Ireland than anywhere else. I wonder why.'

'Must be in the genes. In the DNA.' said Steiger.

'Yes. That's what makes us who we are, I suppose,' replied Gabrin. 'Mine must be pretty mixed. Where my people come from has been the home to so many races over so many centuries.'

They sat back and sipped their drinks.

CHAPTER 33

David and Kate prepared for their expedition to the cliffs and the search for a cave. Clad in drysuits with anoraks over them, they tramped along the old track across the moor unwittingly following the path taken by Gilbert centuries before. The descent into the steep sided dean was tricky but by following the burn to the sea, they gained access to the rocky shore below the cliffs. David had scrutinised the tide tables being well aware of the danger of getting cut off by rising water as they had to skirt the great slabs of greywacke reaching out into the cold sea.

'We must watch our time down here. I don't fancy having to swim round any of these.'

'It's a pity you can't use a kayak. That would be an easier way to get into the bottom of the cliffs.'

'We haven't got time for you to teach me.'

Their progress was slow and laborious. Occasionally they came across a sea cave and ventured in. Most were quite shallow and even the deeper ones were unrewarding. Filled with shingle and rotting seaweed mixed with the flotsam of plastic rubbish, they were malodorous and unpleasant. David was becoming increasingly disgruntled and gave voice to his exasperation with the venture. Kate had been very quiet and seemed in a world of her own.

'I think this is a waste of time.'

There came no reply.

'I said we might as well pack this in. It's useless. None of these caves are likely to have anything in them. If they ever did have, it's long, long gone.'

Kate turned to him.

'Sorry, did you say something?'

'You were miles away. Are you alright?'

'Yes. Just a funny feeling. I seemed to have strange thoughts coming into my head. I can't explain what it was. I could hear your voice, but my mind seemed to be somewhere else.'

'It's probably lack of food. Hypoglycaemia, and the cold, and tiredness. We've hiked a long way to get here and all the climbing. You're needing a rest and something to eat.' said David solicitously.

'There's nothing here,' he added.

Kate looked around and up at the towering cliffs.

'I think there is. I feel there is.'

She put her hands on either side of her head, pressing her palms on her temples.

'I know there is.'

David looked at her. Her demeanour had changed. He had never seen her so intense or with such earnestness in her voice.

'Come on let's get home. The tide is turning. We need to get back up to the dean or we'll get stuck.'

She seemed reluctant to move.

'Come on,' he said then, in coaxing tone, he added, 'We'll come back and try again.'

They made their way back up on to the moor and the old road and thus to the village.

After a scrappy meal, they were both yawning in front of the fire.

David felt Kate was distant and withdrawn. Disappointment, perhaps?

'I didn't think the sea cave idea was a starter,' he ventured.

She said nothing.

'Maybe we've got this figured all wrong,' he added. 'It was all theorising and guesswork. We don't know if the Arrow Stone has any secrets.'

Kate stared into the fire, the light raising highlights in her dark red hair.

'I'm sure there is something there. I could feel it. I don't know what but something.'

'What sort of feeling? Are you sure it wasn't just lack of food? Tiredness?'

'No. It wasn't. I can't describe it.' she replied becoming irritable.

'I'm going to bed.'

David sat by the fire after she had climbed the narrow stairs. He contemplated returning to his own cottage but that would make it seem as if they'd had a row and they hadn't. Had they?

After a while he crept up to the bedroom and, undressing in the dark, slid under the cover beside her sleeping body. Her breathing was rapid and shallow, and she muttered and moaned in her sleep. He put a comforting arm around her and she seemed to settle.

The next morning at breakfast, she was still subdued, not her usual early bird self.

'How did you sleep?' he asked solicitously. He had never asked her such a question before and it made her look at him askance.

'Why do you ask?'

'You seemed to be dreaming. Bad dreams?'

'No. Not bad dreams but voices and a feeling of being lost, not able to find what I was looking for or who I was looking for but at the same time not knowing what or who it was. Anxious feelings.'

She paused, remembering.

'You were in there somewhere and other people. People I don't know.'

She suddenly grinned and shook her head.

'Probably that cheese we used up in the omelettes. We're low on provisions. I'll have to do a supermarket shop.'

'I'd help but I've got a tour today.'

He rose to leave.

'No problem. See you this evening.'

CHAPTER 34

After David left, Kate loitered around the cottage, shuffling notes, making a shopping list, then, suddenly, with purpose, she got into her drysuit, anorak and over-trousers and, collecting her kayaking gear, she packed the torches into a bag and drove to the slipway where the kayak was beached. She had no plan of action, but she knew she had to return to the spot where they had searched below Fast Castle Head. Something was drawing her there.

There was a fair amount of swell and a few white-horse wave tops on the grey North Sea, but she was an experienced kayaker and confident in her ability to cover the three miles or so to the shingle beach below Fast Castle Head.

The current and the wind were against her and she hadn't done any really serious kayaking for months so, by the time she reached her landfall, her muscles and joints ached and she felt very tired and, as she looked up at the cliffs towering above her, very alone. She hadn't been aware of how much she had become used to David always being alongside her.

She shook herself and moored the kayak on a long line. A few stretches and she felt easier and ready for... what exactly? She didn't have any real plan of action. She had just felt compelled to return to that spot.

She clambered over the rocky outcrops and mentally ticked off the caves that they had explored together. She was beginning to feel a little foolish and regretting her impulse and was not looking forward to the journey back when she noticed the little opening at the bottom of a great slab of greywacke tilted against its neighbour. A squat, black triangle just over a metre high and a metre and a half across the base. Kate squatted down and peered in. The shaft from the entrance appeared to slope slightly upwards for some distance. The torch beam showed a passage back into the base of the cliffs. Putting on her head torch and holding the other out in front, she squirmed through the narrow opening and was relieved to find there was slightly more room to move once she was clear of the entrance. It was still a tough crawl up the slope to the rear of the cave with the claustrophobic presence of the surrounding stone walls.

Reaching the end of the long tunnel of the cave, her head torch illuminated the dripping back wall of grey stone. With a sigh of disappointment, she turned on to her side in an attempt to get round to crawl out but the space was too narrow, she would have to shuffle out backwards. In the contortions, her torch flashed upwards and to her surprise, she saw a hole in the roof of the cave that appeared to lead to another chamber above.

Eyes wide with curiosity, she sat up and thrust her head through the opening. Pushing herself with her arms behind her she managed to get her head and shoulders into the upper cave. She realised it was bigger than the passage she was in and levered her arms against the sides to pull herself up into it.

The darkness was absolute. She felt she could almost touch the dense blackness. The torch beam cut through it showing only what it touched with no grey areas. It made it difficult to estimate the size of the chamber but bumping her head on the roof let her know she couldn't stand up. It was either kneeling or, at best, a crouching stoop. She switched on her hand torch and moved it around the walls exploring every inch of the perimeter.

Suddenly, her pulse quickened. There, at the far end, was a shapeless bundle.

She crawled across and found the leather bag left there centuries before, its fabric disintegrating as she handled it. The layers of cere cloth impregnated with beeswax had fared little better, shredding beneath her fingers but the box retained its strength. She cleared the debris of the wrappings and sat with the box between her outstretched legs.

Breathing in short gasps, her heart beating with excitement and with a feeling almost amounting to dread at what she might find, she ran her fingers around the lid feeling for a catch. There appeared to be no lock but the lid would not open. Grimacing in frustration, Kate lay down to look closely with her head torch. The darkness made it difficult to examine the box but, as she held it up to eye level and moved the beam of light along the edge of lid, she saw the little discrepancy in the beading and slid the hidden lever along to elicit a feeling of give under her fingers. Holding her breath, Kate lifted the lid and opened the coffer closed with a prayer by Gilbert centuries before. She lifted out the silver mounted skull and stared into the face of the long departed Watcher. The sightless eye sockets stared back. Her hands trembled as she held it up into the beam of the head torch. The light flowing through it projected weird shadows on to the cave wall behind creating a distorted black counterpart to the gleaming white of the skull. She couldn't look away. Her breathing became shallower and more rapid. Her head swam as voices and images clashed and mingled in her mind. Carefully, almost reverently, she laid the skull on the floor of the cave and, unable to think, she curled up on her side with hands clasped to her temples. She drifted into what the Scots would call a "dwam", a trance-like state, a waking dream.

How long she lay there she wasn't sure but eventually, she gained control of her thoughts and was able to place the skull back in its sandalwood, lined resting place and, shivering with the cold, she crawled to the hatch-like opening to descend into the tunnel beneath.

It took a minute for the sound to register on her still stupefied brain but as her thoughts cleared, she felt a chill of fear. The sound was the rush of sea on shingle. In her dream-like state she had lost track of time and the tide had turned. The waves were now rushing up the narrow sea-cave passage which would soon be under water.

Panic welled up in her throat. The passage was too narrow to swim along and crawling the length of it, underwater, against the in-rushing tide was impossible. She was cursing her impetuosity in coming to this spot unaccompanied and without even telling David where she was going. To be drowned in this stone prison because of her own stupidity brought tears of regret and despair. She cursed the skull and how it had drawn her there. She remembered the words that Gabrin had found in his manuscript about "a secret" being "underground" in "a cave... or a tomb". Was this to be her tomb? She had been so stupid.

Then, slowly, reason returned. The box had lain undisturbed for centuries so even at high water, the upper cave must remain dry. She had only to wait for the tide to turn for her exit to clear. Her shoulders shook as she gasped with relief. It would be about six hours between high tide and low tide, but she needn't even have to wait that long. The water in the cave was at the height of the tide. It only had to ebb enough for the entrance to be clear to let her crawl out. She reckoned there was plenty air in the cave to last.

No danger of asphyxia so, switching off her torches to ensure light when she needed it, she curled up again on the cave floor to await the pull of the moon on the waters rescuing her from her dark cell. Even in the velvety enclosing darkness behind her closed eyelids, the blanched whiteness of the skull with its compelling orbits was there in her mind's eye, holding her gaze. She curled up closer like a foetus, in the darkness of a womb, waiting to be born.

CHAPTER 35

'It's there, my esteemed friend. It's most definitely there.' exclaimed Steiger, clapping his palms together.

'The stone? You've seen it?'

'Yes, indeed.'

'Tell me. How did you find out?'

Gabrin and Steiger had met once more in the country house hotel, in what had once been the library of the long deceased laird of the estate, his fields and woods now dispersed to pay the death duties of previous governments, his house now a hotel and his study where he had received the reports of his factor, a book-lined retreat for guests to have private conversations.

'It was so easy,' explained Steiger.

'I knew Morton's girlfriend lived in St Abbs, so I just drove down there and asked around. There aren't many attractive redheads in a village that size. I even found out her name. As soon as I mentioned her, the guy said "Oh you mean Kate Donaldson". So, of course, I said, "Yeah that's her". I tell you folk around here are so friendly. So trusting.'

He laughed as he recalled the afternoon.

'I made out that I was an old acquaintance from a time she spent in the States come to look her up.'

'Did she spend time in the States?'

'I've no idea but I reckoned I could wing it if anyone enquired further but there was no need. Guys notice striking girls like that. When I asked if anyone knew where she lived, one of them pointed out her house and I just knocked on the door. I had another story for when she answered. I was going to claim that it was all a mistake and she wasn't the person I thought she was but there was no need. The door wasn't even locked. There was no-one there, so I just walked in and had a look around.'

'And the Arrow Stone?'

Steiger grinned triumphantly and passed his phone to Gabrin.

'Yep. It was right there. Here, I took some pictures. It's not much to look at. A few chisel marks on a lump of stone. You can definitely see the arrow carving, but the rest doesn't amount to much.'

'I agree,' said Gabrin.' I too had expected something a bit more elaborate.'

Steiger continued his tale.

'They had obviously been working on it. There were drawings and bits of maps and outlines. They must think they have cracked what it means.'

Gabrin's interest, which had been somewhat diminished by the pictures of the stone, rose.

'Do you think they might have worked out what the secret is that the code in the letter refers to?'

Steiger grimaced.

'I don't know. I didn't have much time. The maps and drawings all seemed to be about a stretch of coastline. It didn't mean much to me, but I did see the name Fast Castle on one of the maps with a circle drawn round it.'

Gabrin thought then spoke.

'So, it would seem that this Castle has something to do with it. I'll google the details. We need to decide what to do next. Do we approach them with an offer, keep a watch on them, or wait and see what develops?'

'OK. We take our time. We check out this castle place. Maybe you should renew your contact with the history guy. Morton. Say you're still interested in whatever line you spun him before. Try and get him to talk a bit. You're good at getting information out of people, or you used to be.'

The reference to Gabrin's reputation as an acquirer and seller of secrets, made them both smile and Steiger called for drinks to seal their continuing partnership.

'By the way, I've had to leave my hotel, so I've rented a cottage on a farm. The hotel put me on to it. Most apologetic but they needed the room etcetera, etcetera. The new place suits me better actually. I can come and go without anyone knowing and it's very comfortable. I reckon it will make the perfect base for operations. Usually does holiday lets but it's a short season and things are beginning to tail off. I spun the farmer the story about family history search.'

Gabrin suppressed a smile as his companion appeared to have dropped the pretence of a family history project. The drinks arrived and Steiger raised his glass.

'Here's to the secret of the Arrow Stone. Whatever it is!'

Gabrin inclined his head in a sign of agreement.

CHAPTER 36

Kate roused herself from her troubled half sleep. Shivering, even in her drysuit, and wet with a combination of condensation and the drips percolating through the rock of the cave roof, she squirmed round and sat up. Her eyes were well adapted to the dark and the first thing she noticed was a faint halo of light at the hole into the lower cave. She crawled over and hung her head and shoulders down through the opening and looked along the tunnel of the lower cave and to her joy could just discern a faint light at the end.

The cave still had water in it, but the level had dropped enough to leave a gap between the surface and the roof. Shivering and shaking with relief and cold. She wrapped the box with its contents in the remains of the coverings and leather satchel and let herself down into the freezing seawater. Pushing the floating box before her, she crawled through the receding tide to the entrance.

As she emerged from the cleft in the cliff, she felt a sense of joy and freedom and suddenly realised how frightened she had been. She started to cry. Silent tears rolled down her cheeks and she just stood, looking up at the sky, her arms clasped round the sandalwood box.

How long she stood on the shingle beach hearing the suck of the ebb tide on the stones and feeling the fresh wind off the sea, she had no idea.

On the wind, she heard a voice, then more voices, calling her name

'Kate. Kate.'

She saw a RIB, a rigid inflatable, edging slowly towards the shore, her kayak bobbing astern. Someone was standing in the bow shouting and waving his arms. It was David.

The RIB crunched on to the edge of the beach and David leapt out. He rushed forward and clasped her in his arms.

'Thank God. Oh, thank God. We found your kayak drifting down the coast. I thought I'd lost you.'

He hugged her closer to him. She said nothing. She just stood holding the sandalwood box close within her folded arms.

'What happened? Where have you been?' said David, then, looking at her drawn face, he spoke gently.

'Let's get you home.'

Hands reached out to help her into the inflatable and someone put a blanket over her shoulders. She sat hunched in the stern as the outboard motor roared them back towards harbour. David sat beside her, his arm protectively round her shoulders.

Just once she turned and looked at him.

'I found it,' she said quietly.

He looked at the box and, as if anticipating a move from him, she half turned away guarding her find with her body. David raised his eyebrows in puzzlement then, with a shrug of acceptance, he held her steady from the motion of the rescue craft.

Back at the harbour, more willing hands helped her climb the iron ladder up the harbour wall. The blanket covered the box and if anyone noticed it, no-one mentioned it.

'Thank you. Thank you. All of you. We're so grateful. I don't know what we would have done...' David's voice broke with emotion.

Kate raised her eyes to the group of well-wishers.

'Yes. Thank you. Sorry to have caused so much trouble.'

'Nae bother, lass. Jist glad tae see you safe.' said the lifeboat crewman.

Then, turning to David.

'Take her hame. Warmth and rest is what she needs. Go on now. Dinnae stand aboot here gettin' frozen.'

'Yes,' he said. 'Yes. We'll get back home now. I'll see you all in the morning.'

He took Kate by the arm and led her back to the cottage. She walked silently beside him, her head bowed as if in prayer.

She sat in the armchair still cocooned in her blanket while he busied himself fuelling the stove and brewing cups of tea. He wasn't very sure if hot sweet tea was the correct remedy, but it was traditional. He resolved not to question her but to wait until she was ready to give her own account.

Eventually, she spoke. She looked steadily into his face and said, 'I'm so sorry for causing all this trouble. I should have told you, but I just had to go back. I don't know why but I just knew it was there.'

'You're safe now that's the main thing. And this?'

David gestured at the box still covered with the blanket. Almost shyly, Kate drew back the edge and held up the box.

'It was in the cave. Another cave. One we'd missed. A small one, with a long passage and another cave above it. That's where I found it, and the tide came in, and I couldn't get out.'

The words came tumbling out. She began to shake with great sobs as the memory of the darkness and the claustrophobia of the stone walls that had trapped her came flooding back.

'There now. There's no need to speak if it's too much just now. It can wait,' David said.

'No. I want to tell you.'

Kate gathered herself and recounted how she had entered the cave and crawled along the passage and found the upper chamber, how she had found the box wrapped in its coverings.

'The next bit is a bit confusing. I'm not sure what happened. I sort of blacked out. I don't know how long for but the tide turned and filled the passage with water and I just had to lie and wait until it ebbed so I could get out.'

'It must have been terrifying,' said David.

'I kept telling myself that if the passage was open when I went in, it had to get clear again, but it was difficult to hold onto that thought. I did panic a bit. I was frightened.'

David leaned towards her, kissed her cheek and held her for a moment. She looked up at him and smiled.

'...But I found it.'

She held the box up.

He decided this was the moment.

'Can I see it?'

She paused for the briefest of moments, her grip tightening, then, looking into his face, she relaxed and said,

'Of course.'

He took it from her grasp, feeling the slight reluctance as she relinquished her hold on it.

He tried the lid.

'There's a sliding catch. There, just under the edge.'

He opened the lid and took the skull out. He noticed Kate's eyes never left it. He could sense the tension in her as she leaned forward in her seat.

'So this is what the Arrow Stone was all about. That Gabrin chap mentioned a skull when he was quizzing me about the Arrow Stone. This is "the secret of the order". I wonder why it was so important.'

He held up the silver mounted relic of the Watcher; of Yaranqash; of Odo de Armand and Jaques de Molay,

The glow from the fire in the stove cast its shadow on the white walls of the cottage. Kate shivered, remembering the shadows cast by her torch beam on the cave wall.

She shifted her attention from the skull to David's face, searching his features for a reaction but he remained his usual calm self.

'It's a funny shape. I'm no anatomist but that's not the shape of a normal human skull.'

Kate ignored the implied question.

'Do you feel anything?' she asked.

'Feel anything?' he replied. 'No. I'm not sure what you mean.'

'Oh, nothing,' she said. 'Here, let me put it back in its box.'

He handed it back to her and she placed it reverently back in the place where it had rested for centuries.

He noticed she kept the box on her lap, her hands resting on the lid.

'Come on. You must be exhausted. Bed and sleep. After what you've been through, it's the only answer.'

Kate nodded and let herself be led to her bedroom. David didn't remark on her taking the box with her or her placing it on the bedside table.

As she snuggled under the bed covers, something seemed to occur to her. Raising her head, she said, 'How did you know where to look for me?'

David thought then shook his head.

'I don't really know. Someone in the crowd at the harbour must have suggested we go that way, then, after we found the kayak drifting, we knew we were on the right track. The most important thing is that we did find you.'

He bent and kissed her again as she closed her eyes.

'Mmmmm. Say thanks to everyone.'

He left her to sleep and made his way down to the harbour to return the blanket. A small knot of locals were still there and were soon asking after Kate and how she was. He was thanking them all for their help and well wishes when a small man with a notebook approached him. He was from the local newspaper and had been alerted to the possibility of a story. David kept his version of the incident simple. Kate had been out kayaking and, although experienced, she had become tired dealing with the tidal currents and had put ashore to rest before returning. Unfortunately, her kayak had slipped from her moorings and left her stranded. He asked the reporter through the medium of his newspaper to convey his and Kate's gratitude to all those involved in her rescue. The newspaper man didn't ask about the box so either no-one had noticed, or no-one thought it significant enough to mention. That made things a lot easier. At least that was what he thought at the time.

CHAPTER 37

Steiger phoned Gabrin with his news.

'Pierre. You're not going to believe this. She's in the local paper.'

Gabrin failed to grasp his meaning.

'Who is she?'

'Morton's girl. Kate whatsername, Kate Donaldson. She was rescued from a...'

He paused while he adjusted his reading glasses.

'...a kayaking accident. She was marooned on rocks or something on the coast near...'

He paused again.

'...Fast Castle.'

His listener interrupted his flow.

'Is this significant?'

'I think it is,' replied Steiger.

'You recall when I got into her cottage, there was a pencil drawing. An outline of the coast with the name Fast Castle scribbled alongside it. I reckon she was looking for whatever the Arrow Stone points to and that was Fast Castle. It all fits.'

He paused waiting for a reply from Gabrin.

'I suppose you could be right.'

'Right? You know I am, and what's more I'm just getting my head round the geography of this area and this Fast Castle place is close to the cottage I'm renting. Real close. Why don't you come up and we can take a look?'

'What's the point? If the girl has discovered the hiding place mentioned in the code. If that's what the Arrow Stone meant, and we don't even know if that's what it was for. If she has found anything, she will have taken it back with her. Or a sample if it's something big.'

Steiger thought for a moment.

'Yeah, you're right. There was no picture in the newspaper so no way of knowing if she was carrying anything. Still, come over and we'll take a look. We can figure out the next move. Do we approach her or both of them directly? We could just ask them and offer money. Think about it on the way over.'

Gabrin put his mobile into his pocket and prepared to leave. He did not like cliffs and caves and did not entirely trust his companion. He paused and put his hand to his jacket over his heart. He felt the comforting outline of a small Kahr P380 pistol, its slim shape indiscernible in the immaculate tailoring of the garment. Airport security had never been a problem for Gabrin.

His satnav didn't include remote farm cottages but at least it came up with the farm name and he was able to navigate to Steiger's new accommodation. He was surprised to find it furnished to a remarkably comfortable standard. The term "farm cottage" had led him to expect a more rudimentary dwelling. Glass in hand, the American welcomed him in.

'Sorry, I haven't had a chance to stock up on your fancy booze, but I can run to a rather nice whisky.'

Gabrin shook his head.

'Well, take a seat,' said Steiger. 'This place ain't half bad. There's even a store of logs for the fire. I'm quite settled in.'

They sat on opposite sides of the fire. They had sat opposite one another so often in the past. In hotel lobbies, cafés, bars, barely furnished apartments, safe houses, they had looked across at one another, exchanging information, making deals, neither fully committing himself, neither completely trusting the other.

'What do we do now?'

Gabrin was silent then spoke in slow measured tones almost as though he were speaking to himself.

'You think they, or at least the girl, found something near Fast Castle because of the story in the newspaper. You think this might be the secret referred to in the coded script. Possibly a skull of some sort? This skull, if that's what it is, has some significance. Some power? This power might be useful. Might be able to... to do what?'

He looked at Steiger. He had sounded sceptical. He was beginning to think this whole venture was ridiculous and a waste of time. His initial curiosity about the hidden message in the old manuscript was waning. What am I doing having this conversation in a farm cottage perched on the edge of the North Sea, wasting my time on long dead stories in a country of which I know little and have no interest in? This is a chimera. What possessed me to get into this nonsense, he thought.

He spoke his thoughts in more guarded terms.

'I think we are wasting our time, my old friend. We have allowed our fancy to take hold of our reason. It must be old age that does it.'

Steiger reached across and grasped his wrist.

'I can see this is all a bit pie in the sky but remember it was you who came to me first. There was something in that old letter that intrigued you. I felt it too. Let's give it a little longer. I think we're nearly there.'

Gabrin gave a resigned sigh.

'Okay.'

Steiger stood up.

'Come on, let's take a look at this castle place. It's not far and there's plenty of light yet.'

He made for the door. Reluctantly, Gabrin rose to his feet, looked at his elegant polished shoes and with a slight shrug followed.

When he saw the steep path down the grassy approach to the cliff edge, he became even more apprehensive. This was not the sort of terrain he had been used to, certainly not in the last few years. The final descent to the narrow rock bridge to the castle promontory made him pause.

'There's not much to see, is there?' he noted, taking in the few bits of masonry that had survived siege, attack and deliberate destruction only to succumb to centuries of onslaught by storm-driven rain and wind.

Steiger had clambered up the sloping stone guarding the entrance.

'Come on. Get up here. Get the feel of the place.'

With much misgiving, Gabrin pulled himself up by the rusting chains looped along the edges of the narrow pathway.

'See that little strip of stones down there,' said Steiger. 'I reckon that's where the girl was when she was picked up by the rescue boat. It just couldn't be anywhere else around here and the article said Fast Castle.'

Gabrin peered tentatively over the edge, feeling a tightening in his loins as he looked down to the shore, hundreds of feet below. He did not like heights.

As he stared down, another feeling imposed itself, not quite in his consciousness but more vaguely, somewhere in the back of his mind. A dormant link coded in the nucleic acids of his DNA responded to the traces of a history clinging to the ruins above and the cave beneath. He stood staring at the coastline with the waves crashing on the rocks and a myriad of shifting shapes and sounds, some like voices but with no discernible words, others like pictures changing form melting into each other, passed through his mind. He felt faint.

'Come on.'

Steiger's voice broke into his reverie.

'We better get back. It's starting to get dark. I don't fancy that path when I can't see where I'm going.'

He turned to where Gabrin was still standing gathering his scattered thoughts.

'Are you alright?'

'Yes, yes. Just coming.'

He clambered back down the sloped stone and across the narrow spit of the entrance path without touching the guard chains. Steiger looked back at him with a puzzled expression, then turned to the task of getting his large frame up the steep slope towards the moor. Gabrin followed, scarcely aware of any effort in the climb or of his ruined shoes.

Back in the cottage, Steiger again asked his companion if he felt alright.

'It's just that you seemed a bit... preoccupied, back there.'

He chose his words carefully gauging the reaction.

'It's nothing. I just felt... I don't know... a bit...'

He searched for the word. How had he felt on that promontory in the ruins above the site of the cave?

'...faint. No. A bit overcome. I think that's the word. Probably just the effort of getting there. I'm not getting any younger. I don't like heights. Maybe it was just that.'

His voiced tailed off somewhat almost bashfully. The truth was he had no idea what had come over him. Steiger had his own way of dealing with the situation.

'What we both need is a drink. You'll have to make do with whisky.'

He poured two generous portions and they sat once again on either side of the fire. Gabrin nursed his between his hands. Steiger took a gulp of the golden liquid and spoke, 'I think we approach them. Tell them we know about their discovery. Offer them money. If it is a means of psycho-telepathy or whatever, a means of... what's the word... scrying that the guy was on about in the old files.'

He saw Gabrin's sudden look of interest.

'Oh, I forgot to mention that I turned up this file from the old Cold War days when they were investigating telepathy and other psycho stuff and there is one mention of a skull as a means of achieving this. It was discounted then, maybe rightly so. On the other hand, if this *is* the skull that was talked about, it would be of interest to the department.'

Gabrin put down his untouched glass.

'In what way, "of interest"? You mean that your department might be prepared to pay for it?'

Steiger was caught slightly off guard by the directness of the question. He was, after all, an employee of the aforementioned department, not an independent agent like Gabrin.

'Well let's just say I would like to obtain the object for further evaluation, under controlled circumstances. Any assistance by yourself in the furtherance of this aim would be, as usual, well compensated.'

This parody of the language of a business contract was accompanied by a conspiratorial grin. Steiger's eyebrows were raised, seeking confirmation of the agreement between them.

Gabrin looked at him and shrugged.

'Okay. I'll stick around for a while to see what transpires. I will expect the fee to be commensurate with my time and effort, and for the sourcing of the information.'

'Done.' said the American. 'We'll contact them in the morning. Both of them or the girl on her own. I hope my hunch is correct and they have found it.'

Gabrin stared into the middle distance for a moment.

'I feel sure they have,' he said quietly.

CHAPTER 38

'I don't know either. I'm not sure what to do.'

This sudden unexpected statement from Kate startled David from his reverie. He turned and looked at her in mild astonishment.

'You were wondering what to do next,' she continued. 'What do we do with it?'

'Well, yes. As a matter of fact, I was wondering what the next step would be.'

Kate sat with the box on her knees, her forearms curved possessively around it. She looked at him directly, almost defiantly.

'I think I... we... should keep it for the time being. It needs a lot of thinking about. What to do. No-one knows about it. It's still our secret.'

She tilted her chin up, as if in a challenge to him to disagree.

'Sure, no need to rush things,' he said in placation. 'As you say, no-one knows about it.'

She nodded, satisfied with his answer, and carried the box with its contents back to the bedroom where she had kept it beside her since her rescue.

David watched her as she left. He was puzzled. He hadn't known Kate for long but he thought he understood her, yet she had changed since the box had come into their possession. The box, in his internal monologue he always used the term "the box" not "the skull" as he still didn't like to think of the contents separately, seemed to have affected her. She often anticipated his words, answering questions before he asked them and her previously effervescent, joie de vivre seemed subdued as though she had some burden on her mind.

He wasn't sure of the status of their find. Was it treasure trove? The silver mounting around the skull seemed genuine and the undoubted antiquity of the thing must give it some value.

Should they inform the National Museum or local government or even the landowner and was that the Crown if it was on the foreshore?

He was pondering these slightly abstruse questions when Kate reappeared.

She looked at him and said quietly but firmly.

'It stays here meantime. No-one knows it's here.'

She paused as if listening.

'I'm sure nobody knows but us.'

She smiled, put her arms round his neck and kissed him.

'Don't worry. Everything will be fine.'

David remained slightly nonplussed by the situation, but Kate seemed determined so, as was his nature, he let sleeping dogs lie. No point in arguing especially as he hadn't a clue what to do next anyway. Now that they, or rather Kate, had found the skull, they had unravelled the secret of the Arrow Stone and now he had a feeling of anti-climax. This wasn't a national treasure hunt for a prize. No-one except themselves even knew it existed. All the effort, the searching and puzzling had brought them to what exactly?

Kate's feelings were very different. Holding the skull seemed to expand her mind, her universe. She was conscious of a stream of images and feelings most of which she didn't understand but which she was gradually coming to terms with. She found she was aware of David's thoughts before he spoke. It was not as though she could "read his mind" whatever that meant. It was simply an awareness of thought in a nebulous wordless image. It took some getting used to. Initially, she thought that David could feel her thoughts too, but it soon became evident that he had no conception of what she experienced. She decided that he wouldn't understand so she kept the "skull effect" as she had nicknamed it, to herself.

She was also aware of another. Especially in that hypnagogic slumber preceding sleep or in the drowsiness of wakening, she could feel another voice, another mind, just beyond the edges of comprehension. A mind like hers. It troubled her but, try as she might, she could not focus on it. It remained just out of reach.

CHAPTER 39

Steiger and Gabrin met at Steiger's rented cottage to formulate a plan of action. Steiger was all for a direct approach.

'We tell them we know they've got whatever secret the letter was about, whatever the stone led them to. It seems to be a skull, or something represented by a skull. Important enough for someone to go to great lengths to hide but to try and leave a message as to where it was. We just say we know they have it and that we want to buy it. Simple.'

Gabrin mulled the suggestion. On the face of it, he couldn't see any objections, but it was not his usual style and he cavilled at the bluntness of it.

'What if they deny it? How do we know about it? What do we say we want it for? We have to have a background. Something plausible or they will be suspicious.'

Steiger spread his big hands wide.

'The truth, or at least some of it, is a good basis, I've always found. It's best to build a story round the truth. We can leave out the bits we don't want to tell them and just dress up the rest. We are business partners who deal in antiquities. You have an interest in old manuscripts. You were following up on one you had come across which seemed to mention a skull. No need to mention ciphers or my department or any of that stuff. A simple tale but basically true. How do we know about it? Oh, it was mentioned by one of the guys who were around at the time the girl got rescued. That's when we reckon she found it.'

'But no-one made any comment. There was nothing in the newspaper report,' interjected Gabrin.

'But they can't be sure that no-one said anything. If we say we heard it that way then they'll naturally assume someone saw something.'

'Sounds reasonable,' agreed Gabrin reluctantly.

He had been less of his usual assured self recently. Ever since his visit to the precarious perch of Fast Castle, his mind had been unsettled. At first he had ascribed it to the feeling of vertigo he had experienced looking down to the inlet below the keep, the inlet where Kate had discovered the box with its contents. Since that time, he had had strange dreams and a feeling of detachment. He was out of his customary milieu. He was a creature of the Mediterranean sun or of the comforting enclosed embrace of the cities. He found this exposed craggy shoreline of the North Sea disquieting. He would have preferred to forget about the whole venture and write it off as a misjudged business venture, but something held him. There was a feeling, a need in him that he couldn't explain.

'What do we do with the skull if that's what it is?'

He looked at Steiger trying to gauge whether the answer was part of a genuine plan or if he was just being strung along.

'I guess the Department would be interested in it. There aren't the funds for left-of-field projects that there used to be, but they would pay your fees and, if it proved useful, there would be a subsequent...' He searched for a suitable word, '...retainer, to keep it to yourself.'

Gabrin nodded in apparent agreement but decided there and then that if he got his hands on the skull, he was not going to meekly hand it over to Steiger's employers even in return for his usual steep fee, but he would go along with the American for the present. He couldn't explain it even to himself, but the skull and possession of it, was becoming more and more important to him.

'Agreed then.' said Steiger. 'We pay them a visit tomorrow. It's time we wrapped this all up. I've used up a huge amount of leave coming over here. I've had to call in a few favours in the department and my wife isn't too happy about this family history story. I reckon she thinks I'm chasing some woman.'

He snorted derisively. 'As if!'

He meshed his fingers and shook his clasped hands together as if he were about to roll dice.

'I didn't anticipate this developing into anything, I was just a little curious but now it's so close, I feel lucky.'

'I think it might just be so,' murmured his companion, guarding his own thoughts.

CHAPTER 40

David and Kate were lolling in armchairs by the stove like cats luxuriating in its warmth. Kate became aware of a presence, a shadow falling across her thoughts. Within a few minutes, there was a knock at the door.

'Who on earth...?'

David sat up, roused from his near slumber.

'Don't answer it,' said Kate. 'They'll go away.'

'Come on. It could be anything or anyone. Maybe it's important. Work or someone needing help. We can't just ignore them.'

Kate curled herself up in the chair, clasping her knees in her arms. She didn't want to meet the person and the mind on the other side of the door.

David answered the knock and was surprised to find the two men on the doorstep.

Steiger introduced themselves with an apology, and an exaggeration of his accent. He somehow felt this added authenticity to his pretence of being a dealer seeking an artefact.

'Ah'm real sorry to intrude on your good selves at this hour but my partner and I would like to discuss a business matter with you and we felt a direct approach was the best way forward. To come and meet with you face to face.'

He stepped back slightly and indicated Gabrin with an open-handed gesture.

'Mah business associate, Monsieur Pierre Gabrin. Ah believe you two have met. May we come in?'

David was taken slightly aback, but his innate friendliness overrode any concerns.

'Well, yes. I don't see why not.'

He stepped to one side.

'Come in.' he said and, over his shoulder, added, 'Kate, we have visitors.'

Kate watched over the top of her knees as the two men entered the room.

'Good evening. Apologies for coming to see you like this without contacting you first, but you're mighty difficult to get a hold of. You seem to be out most of the time.'

This was a shrewd line from Steiger. It was the sort of comment that it was difficult to disagree with but implied that they had been trying to make contact with the young couple.

It gave them a plausible reason for just turning up on the doorstep.

'I suppose we are. We both have work to do. Sorry you couldn't reach us. What can we do for you?'

David's usual politeness took over. Kate said nothing. She continued to view the incomers over the protective wall of her bent knees.

Gabrin inclined his head in reply to David's little speech of welcome but he also said nothing.

His eyes met those of Kate and hers widened in fear. She knew then what the presence was in the back of her mind. The shadow that had been there for several days since she handled the skull. It was Gabrin.

Gabrin himself suddenly grasped what had been troubling him from the time he looked down on the inlet below Fast Castle. He was aware of Kate as a projection in his brain. He could plainly see her, but he could also feel her presence. It was disconcerting but, not without difficulty, he kept his usual bland exterior, his face never betraying the turmoil in his mind.

Kate, too, was undergoing a battle as she clung to her thoughts, her instinctive dislike of the intrusive fusion of minds welling up inside her. She hugged her knees closer up to her chin.

Steiger and David were completely unaware of this struggle as they exchanged pleasantries.

'Let me get down to business,' said Steiger, glancing across to his companion.

A flicker of annoyance crossed his face at Gabrin's apparent inattention, and his tone sharpened slightly.

'We, that is my partner and I,' he continued with emphasis, 'are interested in acquiring an artefact. A historical object which we believe you have discovered. You recall my colleague, Monsieur Gabrin asking you about a skull some time ago? Yes? Well, we would like to purchase the one you found.'

As Steiger had calculated, the direct approach wrong-footed David completely. Until that moment he thought that no-one knew of the skull but himself and Kate. Taken aback, he cast about for an answer and turned to Kate for support, but she was still locked in the struggle to free her thoughts from the intrusion of Gabrin who, in turn, was coming to terms with a situation that, though he did not understand its origins, might have its uses. Both their faces retained their masks of normality.

While the two were locked in their silent mental wrestling match, Steiger continued his conversation with David pausing between each statement.

'The sum involved might be quite a decent amount, possibly running to several thousand dollars, or pounds, or euros. Just state your preference. It could be paid into any bank, anywhere.'

At each pause, he studied the younger man's face for a signal of acceptance or even interest that he could use to advantage to press for a deal. Both were unaware of the significant lack of participation from the other two occupants of the room.

David was searching for the best response he could think of when Kate interjected. Her tone was expressionless, harsh even, as she strove to blank her thoughts from intrusion.

'We have no idea what you are talking about. Who said anything about us having a skull or any other bones? Nonsense. You've been misinformed. Someone's been having you on.'

Steiger and David turned in unison to look at her, now sitting upright in the chair.

Steiger noted the determined set of her features. David noted her use of the inclusive pronoun "we". She was obviously taking control of what had been a dialogue between the two men.

Steiger was used to making quick assessments of any given situation and he realised that further negotiations were useless at that point. He smiled pleasantly and raised his hands palms outwards in a gesture of conciliation, ignoring the rebuff in her reply.

'We'll leave it for the time being. It's all come a bit out of the blue. We'll let you youngsters talk it over. We'll call again when you've had time to think it through.'

His last sentence was addressed directly to David.

During the entire exchange Gabrin had remained silent. He was still trying to analyse the experience of his telepathy or whatever it was with Kate. He couldn't understand it, but he recognised the advantage it gave him over Steiger. The skull was not going to the American's "department". He, Gabrin, was starting to see the implications of his possessing it. What of the girl? She too understood the potential of the skull. He smiled slightly at her rapid and fierce denial of its existence. The two of them, would make a formidable team. The three of them if they included the skull. He had felt its presence even more strongly than before. He knew they had it and he meant to have it for himself.

Steiger made to leave but Gabrin paused for a moment trying to reach into Kate's thoughts but she seemed to have mastered the art of shielding them from him. He nodded in a signal to her. She indeed would be a worthy partner instead of this oaf of an intelligence man.

As they made their way back to the hire car, Steiger said,

'They have it. Whether it's in the cottage or elsewhere I'm not sure but we'll give them a night to think it over. The guy, what d'yuh call him, Morton, seemed to be interested when I mentioned cash but the girl shut him up quick. She's gonna be the problem I reckon.'

Gabrin murmured his agreement.

'Okay. We see them again tomorrow and if they're not there, we take that cottage apart.

If the girl takes charge it's gonna cost a lot more,' he concluded.

More than you can imagine, thought his companion.

After the two men left, David and Kate sat in silence. Neither knew quite what to say, how to start the discussion they both knew they had to have. Kate could feel David's unease, his searching for the most appropriate opening. She spared him the effort.

'They can't have it,' she stated baldly.

'Yes,' he replied. 'But, what do we do with it? Is it ours to keep? Should we hand it over to someone, a museum or...' He broke off and thought for a moment.

'There will be an archaeology department in the local council. They keep an eye on any developments or finds. Perhaps we should contact them.'

'No,' said Kate. 'It stays with me. With us.'

They fell silent again. David felt he had reached an impasse. He tried another approach, one that he knew was the wrong one as soon as he started on it.

'The big chap mentioned money. He said it could be worth several thousands of dollars, or pounds.'

Kate flashed him a look of anger and scorn. David immediately retreated. As he had formed the words he had regretted it.

'Sorry,' he said. 'That was crass of me.'

He knew Kate was possessive of, or maybe even possessed by the skull, and that it had some sort of effect on her, but it was completely outside his experience. He just couldn't understand it or her.

The Arrow Stone itself had been his original interest. A curious anomaly among the many cup and ring marked stones that had been his hobby to find and record. He had been, by his own admission, a bit of an anorak. Identifying the elusive stone mentioned in the annals of an Edwardian historical society, had seemed like a pleasant way to explore the countryside where he had come to live. He had not expected to find a beautiful girl or to get involved with coded messages and an ancient skull that seemed to have strange effects on people and to be sought after by others. He felt a bit out of his depth. Finding the Arrow Stone had been a bit of fun, a puzzle, a quest like a kids' treasure hunt and it had been a great way to spend time with Kate. She had been an enthusiastic partner, keen to get the reward, to follow the clues, be the first to find the Easter egg or the hidden sweets.

Since she had found the prize, the enthusiasm had changed to a steely determination to hold on to it. The bubbly laughing Kate that he had first met had been replaced by a quieter, more remote copy.

'Don't worry about me.'

Kate's voice broke into his reverie. He looked across at her. She was smiling at him.

'I'm fine. Honest, I am. That pair did knock me off my guard a bit, I will admit, but I'm okay now.'

'I wonder how they knew about what we found, what you found. Why do they want it?'

'I don't know but they're not getting it,' said Kate.

CHAPTER 41

The next day, Kate thought long and hard about the skull and its influence. She felt a weight of responsibility for its safety. Like all the others over the millennia who had had the skull in their keeping, rather than possessing it, she was possessed by it. She was certain that she could not allow Steiger and, in particular, Gabrin to have it. She knew that Gabrin shared with her the powers conferred by it, but she felt no kinship to him. She felt his motives for its use were malign.

David did not seem to understand the significance of it. He obviously was not able to use its resource to see into the thoughts of others. He was reliable and Kate knew he would do anything she asked of him, but she felt she had to deal with the problem on her own. After much consideration, she concluded that the only way was to return it to the cave where she had found it. She reasoned to herself that it had lain undiscovered for centuries in its secret chamber before, by luck, she had brought it out. No-one else had crawled up that watery tunnel since Gilbert's day and even David didn't know exactly where she had been before she had been rescued from the shore with her prize.

She resolved to return to the cave and hide the skull again.

In place of the cerecloth wrappings and leather bag that Gilbert had used in the fourteenth century, she used polythene and gaffer tape and a nylon stuff bag to protect the sandal wood box from the elements. She intended to drive out to the Dowlaw and make her way down the dean to the foreshore and then over the rocks to the shingle beach, the path taken by Gilbert all those centuries before. She was putting the stuff bag with its precious contents into the boot of her car when it dawned on her that she had to be there at low tide to access the cave.

She walked down to the snug little harbour with its surrounding cluster of houses. She picked her way between parked cars, stacks of lobster creels, coils of rope and all the impedimenta of a working fishing harbour to find the wooden hut that grandly proclaimed itself as the Harbour Master's Office. There she found the pinned notices of the times of high and low water. She would have to get to the cove at low tide to gain entrance to the cave and thus to the upper chamber. The next low tide was late evening. David had said his last trip was down the coast and he would be some time in getting back. She had decided to make the trip alone. Having experienced both her ability to see into his mind and witnessed Gabrin's tussle with her own thoughts, she decided the less he knew, the less he could inadvertently disclose.

She reckoned her kayaking gear would afford sufficient protection for the long crawl up to the back of the cave and the access to the hidden chamber. She was returning to her cottage to put on a drysuit and suitable gloves and boots when she saw the car half hidden between two larger vehicles in the upper car park but with the unmistakable figures of Steiger and Gabrin inside.

CHAPTER 42

After their rebuff by Kate and David, the two men had discussed their next move. Without disclosing the interaction of minds with Kate which had increased his desire to own the skull, Gabrin had suggested that they return to negotiate further.

He suggested that David had seemed to be swayed somewhat by the idea of a price for it.

Steiger dismissed this as unlikely. They were not going to come to a deal given Kate's implacable opposition.

'She’s not gonna change her mind and he, sure as hell, ain't gonna change it for her.'

Gabrin had to admit that this was the most likely scenario unless he admitted to Steiger the effect the skull had on him and this he was loath to do. Increasingly, he was becoming disenchanted with his associate. A feeling of superiority, a disdain was settling on him. The skull seemed to have differing effects on the minds of those it affected. As the base material on which it worked varied so did the changes it wrought as its users had found in the past. It not only gave powers, it also made demands on the character of those on whom these were bestowed.

Steiger's blunt approach was simply to burgle the cottage and seize the skull.

'After all, who are they gonna inform? They're not the owners. Nobody knows about the thing.

Do they go to the cops and admit they found it and kept it? No, of course they don't. Even if they did, who'd believe such a crazy story?'

Despite the lack of subtlety, Gabrin had to concede the logic of his argument. They decided to keep a watch on the cottage and seize their opportunity.

Kate saw the two men, but they were unaware of her. She doubled back and approached the cottage from the other direction. Undetected, she got in the back door to the kitchen. She changed into her kayaking outfit and, taking a torch and the bag with its precious contents, she let herself out of the same door and made her way to her car. She decided to drive round the village as though she were going down to the harbour then turn sharply toward the road out to go by way of the moors to Fast Castle.

Steiger and Gabrin saw the little car and felt this was their chance to break into Kate's cottage. Leaving their car, they strode towards it.

Gabrin paused as a stream of images flooded into his mind.

'She's got it with her.' he shouted.

'How do you know?' began Steiger.

'I just know.' replied the other. 'Believe me, I know.'

The big man didn't argue. They raced back to their car.

As she rounded the bend out of the village, Kate caught sight of them in her mirror.

Accelerating out of the village, she sought the coast road and access to the moors. The sky was darkening as the twilight closed in. She could see the lights of the vehicle behind. It occurred to her that if she could swerve off the road and dowse her lights, she could lose her pursuers. She wrenched the wheel round and skidded into the entrance to the track to the lighthouse on St Abbs Head. She shut off the lights and watched in her mirror, holding her breath as the other car raced by the road end. She sat trembling a little as the rear lights faded into the distance.

'She's certainly shifting,' observed Steiger peering ahead.

Gabrin went rigid.

'She's not there!' he snapped. 'She's turned off.'

'What, where?' Steiger turned his head, veering across the road.

'I know she's not ahead of us. Stop. We must turn back,' commanded his companion.

The big American shrugged and looked for an open field gate to reverse into.

'If you say so.'

Kate had just managed to get her rapid breathing under control when she saw the lights over the rise of the road.

With the moors road route cut off, her new plan had been to park her car and make her way on foot to the little cove where she kept her kayak. It was a fair distance but she knew that now she couldn't risk travelling by road even if she had given her followers the slip for the time being. The flash of the returning car lights put paid to that. She couldn't outrun a car.

Starting the motor, she set off along the track to the headland without lights in the half dark.

If I can just get to Pettico Wick, she thought, peering through the windscreen trying to follow the twists of the single track road across the farmland to the Head.

'There! Turn off there,' said Gabrin pointing to the barely noticeable lane branching off under the trees from the main road. Steiger obeyed and swung the car on to the lighthouse road.

'There she is!' shouted Gabrin, as the headlight caught the blacked out car ahead.

Seeing the lights on the rear view mirror, Kate gave up her slow purblind crawl along the twisting track and, turning on her headlights, accelerated away.

She realised her plan to park the car at the cove where it would be clearly seen from the road was a non-starter. Driving across cattle grids and round tight bends she desperately tried to work out an alternative.

Before she could decide on a course of action she had reached the end of the road. Literally, the end of the road. The track stopped at the top of the Head in the lighthouse car park. Grabbing the bag with the skull, she ducked out of the driver's door just as the flash of the following headlight beams reflected from the lighthouse wall.

Grassy paths ran in all directions across the headland. Clutching her bundle to her chest, Kate stumbled down one towards the cliff edge.

St Abbs Head was created by a great outflow of lava from ancient volcanoes, a massive fist thrust into the face of the North Sea, defying the elements to do their worst. Its great knuckles of cliffs towered two hundred feet above the gnawing surge of the waves that tore great bites from them creating fissures and gullies.

She knew of one such sheltered nook. A hidden secret place where she had sat and watched the sun rise through the arch of an eroded outlier on the days when her bird counting had taken her to the Head before the kittiwakes and guillemots had left their roosts. Could she find it along the precarious tracks at the cliff edge?

She could hear the slamming of the car doors behind her.

Steiger and Gabrin looked round, peering into the gathering gloom of the twilight.

'She's here. She can't get far. You take that side, I'll circle round by the road. Shout as soon as you see her.'

The American advanced cautiously along the barely visible sheep track from the car park to the point, his companion with innate distrust of heights kept to the landward side of the circle. They hoped to entrap Kate. They guessed she must be crouching somewhere among the dips and folds of the sheep-chewed pasture covering the rocky ground. There was little or no cover, no hiding place. They felt confident she couldn't get past them.

Kate stumbled on in the twilight gloom, without a plan, uncertain of her next move. She made for Nunnery Point, the furthest out projection of the massive promontory. It was here that the eponymous Aebba, the Northumbrian princess, had come in the sixth century to establish her religious foundation. A place where she would be safe from marauders.

Now, centuries later, another young woman fleeing from pursuers, was seeking sanctuary, Kate could hear Steiger close behind her. He was surprisingly fleet of foot for such a big man. Desperately, she cast her mind back to her time spent along the cliffs during her bird counting expeditions, visualising the scene in her mind's eye thinking of a hiding place. Suddenly she recalled a spot. She was at the pathway as it came to her.

A sharp turn to her right. A short track straight to the edge between two outcrops. A few yards only but with a slight bend that concealed a niche scarcely half a metre deep. It couldn't be seen from the main path. She squeezed herself against the curve of it, clutching her bundle to her, trying to suppress her rapid breathing. She froze trying to meld into the rock behind her. She heard her pursuer's gasps of exertion as he crashed past the end of the path. Her relief turned to fear when he stopped and slowly came back to look down the little gap to the view of the sea and sky beyond.

She heard his feet scuffing on uneven ground. Motionless, she stood as he passed within a few feet of her. Reaching the end, he stopped, took a deep breath and looked out over the edge to the crashing breakers on the Carrs below. He paused, as if hypnotised by the surge of the sea beneath him. Behind him, Kate saw her chance. She eased out of her hiding place and backed as silently but as swiftly as she could towards the main track. Steiger heard the slight sound and spun round. They looked each other in the eyes for a second. As she turned to run, he raised his hand and shouted at her. Whether it was the suddenness of his movement or a gust of wind or the leather soles of his shoes slipping on the tussocky grass, no-one would ever know but over her shoulder Kate heard his shout change to a half scream and when she turned again, he was gone.

He must have fallen backwards over the edge and down two hundred feet to the rocks below and the waiting sea. Kate didn't stop to look or think but ran round the headland to the furthest point then down the scree covered slope above Pettico Wick where her kayak was pulled up on the slipway.

As Gabrin was doubling back by the roadway, he heard the scream of his companion.

Panting with the unaccustomed effort, he reached the car park and shouted for Steiger without response. In the gathering dark, he traced the path along the cliff top calling to the American then eventually realising what had become of him.

His first thought was to get out of the area in case anyone else had witnessed the event. He looked at Kate's car still parked there and shrugged. She seemed to have evaded them. He knew, he knew with certainty, that no damage had befallen her or her burden. The presence of the skull was still there.

He felt only a slight pang of regret at the presumed demise of Steiger. Theirs had been a business arrangement. Their friendship had never been more than that. Mutual self-interest had been their bond and now that was gone. He thought that, with the way things were developing, his feelings about the skull and its effect on him, maybe fate had intervened fortuitously. He had always anticipated a break in the partnership when it came to deciding the destination of the skull. This accident had saved him the trouble. He was now working solo. He had often done so in the past.

As he drove down the road from the lighthouse, his view looked out over the sea as he passed Pettico Wick and there, in the gloom, he could just make out the shape of a kayak being paddled westwards along the coast.

CHAPTER 43

Bent over the bow of her kayak as if dodging bullets, Kate paddled furiously up the coast towards the barely visible Fast Castle. The silhouette of the headland, as if drawn in black ink against the afterglow of the sunset, could just be seen in the encroaching darkness. She realised that she had to get to the cave before high tide. The sandalwood box was carefully stowed, and the little boat skimmed through the waves as she raced against the time, the currents and her own fears. She didn't like the idea of kayaking in the dark with the approach to the rocky shoreline but felt she had no option. She cast her thoughts back to the scream as Steiger had vanished over the edge and shuddered. Her car was still there, abandoned with the keys in it and her mobile lying on the passenger seat. It would be noticed in the morning if not before, yet she had no way of letting David know where she was.

Dismissing it all, she concentrated on the task at hand, the return of the skull to its hiding place.

The moon had risen by the time the bow of the kayak crunched on to the shingle and she was grateful for the light. Mooring was difficult but she secured the craft and retrieved the box from its hull. The moonlight cast weird distorting shadows across the inlet. She stood for moment trying to orientate herself and find the cave entrance amid the many splashes of blackness on the pale grey rocks. She felt the wavelets breaking over her feet and realised that she didn't have much time for the long crawl up to the hidden chamber and back out again before the tide reached its height. The thought of being trapped again in the stone tomb of the upper cave filled her with dread but she felt she must return the skull to its hiding place. She must keep it safe from those such as Gabrin. She had felt his desire to possess it. She would not let him have it.

Searching along the base of the cliffs, Kate flashed her torch into every pool of shadow. She hadn't realised how different the cove would appear in the moonlight and how much each wave-washed rock looked like its neighbour. She told herself she had to find the cave and soon. A race against the tide. She gave a little exulted cry when she recognised the triangle of the entrance beneath the great slab of greywacke.

It was then the voice hit her like a slap across the cheek.

'Good evening, Miss Donaldson.'

Standing above her on a flat rock was Gabrin. His light linen suit, silver-white in the moonlight, gave him a spectral appearance.

Kate stood transfixed. He was in her sight and in her mind. She stared at him. In her sudden confused state, she thought he had his arm extended as if to shake hands then she saw the gun in his hand.

'I knew you would be here,' he said. 'Not an easy place to reach but the car is faster than the canoe. Gave me some time to find the path.

He gestured with the little pistol for her to come to him.

'Come. And bring your cargo with you. We have business to discuss.'

He waved the gun in the direction of the path up the dean to the cliff top. Kate realising that he would have no qualms about gaining possession of the skull without her if necessary, made her reluctant way upwards.

The long climb was undertaken in total silence, but she could feel his presence in her thoughts. She blanked her mind, willing herself to think of nothing, concentrating on each step, on each footfall. She couldn't give him a way in, not even through her anger.

After the trudge up the dean on to the moor, Gabrin shouted to her from behind to go to the right to a tarred road. She looked over her shoulder and noticed with grim satisfaction that he was having difficulty sustaining the pace she had set. He was falling behind. She thought to make a run for it, but his voice cut through her thoughts.

'Stop!'

She stood in the road clutching the box to her.

He caught up and was immediately behind.

'Don't try anything silly. I have no wish to harm you.'

He then gave her the slightest push on the shoulder.

'It's not much further.'

Kate's sullen refusal to speak continued as they walked the last quarter of a mile to a small parking area where Gabrin had left his car, and then on the short distance to the cottage Steiger had rented.

All the time she battled to keep him out of her thoughts by blanking her mind, but this left it numb and unable to formulate any escape plan. She moved as if in a trance.

Gabrin pushed open the door and gestured with his gun for her to enter.

The room was lit by a lamp and the stove was burning. Gabrin had obviously had time to return to the cottage while she had sweated her way along the coast. He pointed to an armchair.

'Do take a seat,' he said in a conciliatory tone.

He sat opposite and laid the gun on a table next to his chair. He inclined his head towards it.

'I'm sorry to have subjected you to such methods. Believe me, they are not my usual way.'

He smiled at her and Kate could feel him in her thoughts. In the presence of the skull, he seemed to be gaining more ability to reach her. She blanked her mind again making a wall, a barrier against him.

'Miss Donaldson.' he purred. 'May I call you Katherine, or is it Kathleen?'

'Katherine,' replied Kate and immediately regretted having spoken. It gave him another tiny advantage in their battle of wills.

'We have much in common. We should be allies not adversaries.'

He nodded towards the box on her lap. She tightened her hold on it.

'I know you have the skull. I know that you are aware of its power, of its effect and I know that you are also aware that I too can access that power.'

Kate remained silent.

'You saw what happened to Steiger?'

'He fell.'

'Yes, I thought so. I didn't think you were capable of...'

His voice trailed off as he looked at her quizzically, inviting a response.

She remained resolutely mute.

'Come now, Katherine. We would make a formidable team. You are a brave, beautiful young woman. I have much experience and many contacts. Think of what we could do with the power the skull gives us.'

He leaned forward towards her.

'You know, I've yet to see it. I know you have it. I can feel it in my mind.'

She tighten her grip on the box

'Relax. I mean no harm, but we are different, you and I, from the others. I felt it at your cottage. Your friend, Mr Morton, he does not understand.'

He paused.

'Nor did Steiger.'

'We *are* different. We belong together.'

Kate was not sure what to make of this approach. She had been taken prisoner at gunpoint yet Gabrin seemed to be wooing rather than threatening her. Her thoughts were confused and she struggled to keep them suppressed.

Gabrin smiled in understanding.

'It's perfectly simple. I do not know the means by which the skull affects us. I know you have it. I am aware of the power it conveys, and I know you too have that power. The manuscript called it the "captor of thoughts". That's what brought me, and Steiger, here. A fourteenth century letter with a coded message about a secret. A message that described the Arrow Stone though it didn't call it that.'

He leaned back again. Kate, despite herself, was interested. Gabrin sensed it and continued.

'You, very conveniently, found the stone for us. I say "us" but then poor Steiger is no longer... interested. So, you see, my dear, the "us" could now be you and me.'

Kate's mind was a whirlpool of emotions, of anger, of revulsion, of fear. She was trying to cope with this when suddenly, with the speed of a striking snake, Gabrin reached across and seized the box from her lap. She sprang forward but his hand went to the pistol and he motioned her back into her seat. She sat back, gripping the arms of the chair. He relaxed a little and replaced the gun on the table allowing him to open the box.

He took the silver mounted relic from its resting place and stood up, holding it in front of him.

Kate sat on the edge of her chair desperate to leap and tear it from his hands. She looked to the gun whereupon he turned as if remembering it, picked up the automatic and slipped it into his jacket pocket.

Gabrin turned the skull of the Watcher round in his hands and looked into the empty eye sockets as others had done before. He could feel the orbits giving access to portals that he couldn't comprehend but he felt compelled to enter.

'So, this is it,' he murmured. 'This is what the old monk was keeping safe from...? From whom or what, I wonder? Where did it come from? Who used it and for what purpose?'

He turned to Kate.

'I don't suppose we'll ever know. What we *do* know, what we can feel, is the power it has. You and I together. We can use that power. Yes, and we can find out what else it can do. What *we* can do. Together we can do so much.'

His voice was rising as he spoke his face becoming animated. Standing in front of the seated girl, he seemed to grow in stature. She felt him towering over her.

Holding the skull up, it caught the light from the lamp and threw its distorted shadow on the wall, the same shadow Kate had seen in the light of her head torch on the wall of the cave.

The same feeling of fear and awe that she had experienced then came flooding back.

He must not have the skull.

She leapt at him and wrenched it from his hands. The force of her challenge threw Gabrin off balance. She ran for the door and out into the night.

CHAPTER 44

David Morton was beside himself with worry. It was late. It was dark. Kate's car had been reported at the lighthouse on the Head, apparently abandoned with the keys still in the ignition. He had gone to the slipway at Pettico Wick and found her kayak gone. In a torment as to her whereabouts, he decided to call the police and coastguard and report her as missing. He did not mention the visit by Gabrin and Steiger or the story of the search for the skull. He still hadn't decided whether to do so or not by the time the police car arrived at Kate's cottage.

The uniformed officer who took the details was accompanied by a man in plain clothes who remained silent. David in his agitated state didn't catch the introduction, if indeed it was given.

He blurted out the details of the missing kayak. The policeman reported on his personal radio requesting that the local inshore lifeboat be launched.

The plainclothes man spoke for the first time.

'You had best come with us, sir.'

He took David by the arm and led him outside. In addition to the police car, there was another vehicle with tinted windows. The man opened the back door and motioned for him to get into the back seat. As David entered, his eyes became used to the dark and he was aware of another occupant. In the other corner was a small figure wrapped in a heavy tweed coat and wearing a fur hat.

'Good evening, Mr Morton.' came the voice from the shadows.

David recognised the measured tone and recalled a previous conversation.

'You. Miss, Miss, I can't recall the name. You were on my tour.'

'The name is Murdison. Yes, I had the pleasure of your excellent guidance but enough of that for the moment. We have hired one of the boats. It usually takes anglers and divers out. The lifeboat is already out searching around the Head but I have an idea where we should be heading.'

The car was already half way down the winding road to the tiny harbour.

They tumbled out of the parked car and down the iron rings on the harbour wall. Miss Murdison showed an agility that belied her years.

David followed unquestioningly. His head was in a spin but he grasped enough to understand that Kate was in some danger and this elderly woman knew how to avert it.

The boat powered its way out of the harbour mouth and headed northwest across the dark sea.

The small group of David, Miss Murdison and her silent companion sat in the stern. No-one spoke until the man whom David assumed had some police role, moved forward and spoke to the skipper at the wheel.

'Another twenty minutes or so, he thinks,' he reported to Miss Murdison who was obviously his superior though in what capacity was unclear.

David was lost for words. There were so many questions he wanted to ask but he didn't know where or how to start and the roar of the engines made conversation impossible. 'Where are we heading?' he managed to shout.

'Fast Castle,' she replied and retreated into the folds of her coat.

A sound carried on the wind, a crack like a pistol being fired.

Miss Murdison spoke to her companion and urged him forward.

He returned and said, 'He says this is as fast as the boat will go.'

The vessel was indeed travelling at some speed bouncing across the waves.

Eventually, in the moonlight, David could make out the distinctive shape of Fast Castle Head. He strained his eyes for a sight of the kayak.

CHAPTER 45

Knocked off balance by the suddenness of Kate's movement, Gabrin stumbled and grabbed the back of the armchair for support. Kate was out the door before he could recover. He ran after her but she was younger and fitter and left him behind as she raced off. He fired a shot into the air to scare her, hoping she would stop but Kate was well ahead back down the path to the shore.

The middle-aged businessman ran after her, unable to catch her but sticking to his pursuit. He fell and picked himself up. He crashed into gorse bushes and tore through them regardless of their spines. He cursed his elegant shoes as he slipped on the moorland grass. He kept on. The desire for the skull drove him. His lungs were on fire, his breath came in great rasping sobs, sweat ran from his brow into his eyes but still he kept on.

His feet crunched on the shingle as he arrived at the beach. He could see the figure ahead launching the kayak.

'Stop!' he cried. 'Stop or I'll fire!'

He held the pistol up where she could see it.

Kate stood still and looked over her shoulder at the man advancing across the beach. She made her decision and turned away pushed the craft out to sea and clambered aboard.

Gabrin fired again into the air and, seeing that had no effect, he ran towards the kayak, splashing knee deep into the water to make a lunge for its stern.

As Kate drove her paddle in, sending the craft lurching forward, Gabrin, waist deep by now, grabbed the back toggle and held on. She paddled with all her strength against the drag of her pursuer and the canoe cleared the shallows and made it out into the current.

Gabrin had pulled himself over the stern and was holding the back of the cockpit. Kate turned and lashed out at him with the paddle. He fended off her swipes and clung on with one hand. The craft was rocking violently, and it took all Kate's skill to keep it upright.

She knocked him off the stern and he grabbed the side of the cockpit, overturning the vessel. Both were flung into the sea. She felt the shock of the icy water as she fought her way back to the surface and clung to the upturned kayak for support.

In the moonlight, she could see the skull, silvery-white, drifting down and away in the current and Gabrin swimming desperately after it. He made one last effort and grasped it as the waters closed over him. He did not surface again.

Despite her drysuit, the numbing cold made Kate feel strangely tired and sleepy. Her grip on the upturned kayak was loosening when David and the plainclothes man wrestled her aboard the launch and wrapped her up.

Back at the harbour, they carried her to the cottage.

'That's twice you've done this,' said David.

Kate smiled weakly.

'I promise. Never again.'

Miss Murdison stood up and assumed her school mistress role again. She spoke as if addressing two pupils caught out of bounds on some escapade.

'Enough for now. We will let the lifeboat crew and coastguards know you are safe. We will discuss this in the morning.'

She indicated her taciturn companion.

'Johnson will remain here tonight, as a precaution.'

She did not elaborate on the reasons for such a precaution. Like two chastened school children, they went to bed. Kate was too exhausted to answer David's questions. She gave him a short account of what had happened, sufficient to stop him asking any more.

'I went to put it back. I didn't want them to have it. Steiger and Gabrin. They chased me. Steiger fell, up on the Head. I got away. I had to put it back. Not to let him have it. Then Gabrin came. He had a gun. He took it from me but I didn't want him to have it. He knew what it could do. Tried to get away in the kayak. We went over. It's gone. He didn't get it. I saw him try but he couldn't...'

'... It's gone.' Her voice trailed off to a whisper.

David held her as they both drifted into sleep.

CHAPTER 46

'You've contrived to spoil my retirement,' said Miss Murdison. 'The pair of you.'

The three of them, Kate. David and Miss Murdison were seated round the table in the cottage. The silent Johnson had departed after his boss arrived.

'Yes, I really have retired and thought this was a quiet spot to spend the rest of my time. I was just absorbing the atmosphere, the feeling of the place. I particularly enjoyed your tour.'

She gave David a slight nod of approval. She still managed to convey the impression of a teacher praising a usually mediocre pupil for a better than expected piece of schoolwork.

'...when all this business started.'

She pursed her lips in mock disapproval.

'Although I am no longer actively involved with the government department where I was employed, I'm still on the reserve list, as it were. They keep in touch.'

'What department might that be?' asked David.

'Oh, security mostly. Making sure the wheels of policy turn smoothly.'

The tone made it clear that that was as much as they were going to be told. The tone that implied that it was grown-up business of no concern to the children.

They sat dutifully in their seats and listened.

'This part of the coast used to be top secret. During the war, it was part of a chain of radar stations giving early warnings of German bombers. In the Cold War, a nuclear-bomb proof bunker was built underground to house equipment to counter the Russians. It was massive. One of several in Scotland.'

She paused and took a sip of tea.

'All miniaturised nowadays. No great machines full of valves and wiring. No feet on the ground. All automatic. Monitor from afar.'

She sipped again and Kate regretted that there were no china cups and saucers in the cottage only mugs. She felt she had let the side down.

Their mentor continued her talk.

'Still, the area is significant. We still keep an eye on it, from a distance.'

She turned and looked directly at them.

'So, when one of whom a famous thriller writer has called "the cousins" turns up in this part of the world supposedly researching his family tree, I get a call from my ex-colleagues asking me to make a few discrete enquiries. I mean, every other American seem to have a Scottish granny but Steiger. That doesn't ring true does it? Then another face with a history shows itself. Monsieur Pierre Gabrin. An old associate of Mr Steiger. The department heard nothing from official sources, so they concluded that the pair were working together but on what?'

'They had a letter, an old manuscript that told them about... about what we found,' interjected Kate.

'Yes, I heard about your search for the Arrow Stone. Is that what you called it?'

'Yes.' said David. 'That was all we were interested in, to start with. Then Gabrin came to me with his story of the manuscript and the skull. We didn't know about that until we worked out the message on the stone.'

'And you found the skull.'

'Yes. Kate did.'

He shuddered at the memory.

'She nearly drowned. I wish we'd never found it, never solved the puzzle, never found the Arrow Stone. It's all my fault with my stupid obsessions.'

Kate put her arm around his shoulder.

'And you, Kate? May I call you Kate? What do you think?' asked Miss Murdison.

'Do you regret finding the skull?'

Kate thought back. She recalled the excitement of solving the riddle of the Arrow Stone, the strange feeling of connectivity she had experienced being near the skull and the mixture of awe, fear and desire for possession she had felt when she held it. The strange power it had given her, the power to understand other's thoughts.

She thought of Gabrin. He too, had wanted to possess the skull and had, like her, become possessed by it.

'No' she said.' I think I was meant to find it. It was as if it found me. Holding it gave me a feeling I've never had before and, I know, I will never have again. It's funny. I can't really say what I feel. I'm glad it's gone but I feel as if part of me is missing. A bit, sort of empty.'

She stared out the window at the grey North Sea that had twice almost claimed her and, in her mind's eye, she could see the ivory white of the skull as it sank beneath the waves.

Epilogue

In the following week, a news item appeared in the local press.

A body recovered from the sea off the Berwickshire coast near St Abbs, was that of Monsieur Pierre Gabrin. M. Gabrin lived in Paris and was a collector of historic documents. It is understood that he was visiting Scotland to research the origins of a manuscript he had recently acquired. M. Gabrin has no immediate family.

It is believed he slipped on rocks near to Fast Castle and was pulled in to deep water by the tidal undertow. It is not known why he was in that particular location but police and coastguards have taken the opportunity to stress the importance of correct footwear and clothing when exploring the shoreline and of being aware of tides and currents. They have emphasised that it is advisable not to go unaccompanied.

The following week another item appeared.

A body washed up on the Berwickshire coast has been identified as Mr Brett Steiger, an American visitor to the area. It is reported that Mr Steiger, from Washington D.C., was holidaying in Berwickshire while researching his family history. The appropriate authorities in the U.S.A. have been informed. Mr Steiger had been seen in the vicinity of St Abbs and it is thought to have fallen while visiting St Abbs Head. A police spokesman said that the cliffs can be dangerous and visitors should be cautious in their approach to them.

And the Skull?

The waters of the North Sea held it as it spiralled down. Down to where the people like the Watcher had once trod, where they had hunted and fished in the rich marshes of Doggerland before the climate changed and the sea overcame the land.

The Atlantic waters washing down from the north create currents down the east coast of Britain. The skull was tossed in the depths like dice from a gambler's hand. To where? Its resting place once more a secret.

Historical Characters

The Knights Templar Poor Fellow-Soldiers of Christ and of the Temple of Solomon. Created in 1129 to protect pilgrims to the Holy Land. They became extremely powerful and wealthy before being dissolved in 1312 after a series of allegations of blasphemy and idolatry.

The Order of St Benedict The Benedictines, the Black Monks, founded in 529. A monastic order throughout Europe, they were given lands for Coldingham Priory in 1100 by King Edgar of Scotland.

Robert I, Robert the Bruce King of Scotland 1274 – 1329. Seized the throne after killing his rival John Comyn in a church, an act for which he was excommunicated. He was victorious in the War for Scottish Independence against Edward II of England.

William Sinclair, Bishop of Dunkeld In 1310 he was one of twelve Scottish bishops to swear fealty to King Robert. He was a strong supporter of the Bruce but after the king's death he switched his allegiance to Edward Balliol who usurped the throne in 1332 when the child king, David II fled to France.

Imad ad-Din Zengi 1085 – 1146 A Turkish atabeg who ruled Mosul, Aleppo and Edessa. He was brought up by Kerbogha, the governor of Mosul. He founded the Zengid dynasty. He was assassinated by his slave, Yaranqash.

Yaranqash According to Damascene chronicler, Ibn al-Qalanasi "... one of Zengi's attendants, for whom he had a special affection and in whose company he delighted... who nursed a secret grudge against him on account of some injury previously done to him by the Atabeg, stabbed him numerous times and then fled."

Odo de Armand Marshal of Jerusalem and Grand Master of the The Poor Knights of the Temple of Solomon - the Templars.

Gerard de Ridefort Grand Master of the Templars.

Philip IV of France 1268 - 1314 "Philip le Bel" Philip the Fair. In 1306, he expelled the Jews from France and, in 1307, he annihilated the order of the Knights Templar. Philip was in debt to both groups.

Jacques de Molay The last Grand Master executed by burning alive as a heretic by Philip IV. Predicted the downfall of the Capet dynasty.